"TEN YEARS AGO WE DIDN'T KNOW THEY EXISTED," SAID MAX.

"A whole empire of human-occupied worlds stretching in from Alpha Centauri toward the galactic center. Five years ago you were only a name on a list. Even a year ago I was ready to start questioning whether we'd been training the right man. An Empire of a thousand worlds, and one little Earth. They forgot us once, and maybe they could forget us again—but not if you're the man who goes in and observes them. You've got some ax of your own to grind with these High-born—"

Jim shrugged. He turned back to his packing and felt his arm violently seized and wrenched as Max tried to turn him around.

Swiftly, this time, Jim turned. He knocked Max's grip loose with the edge of his right hand, then laid that same hand so that the thumb touched Max's neck behind the angle of his jawbone; and it pressed in tightly.

Max's face whitened, and he gasped. "You— you're a fool! You'd kill me?"

"If I had to," said Jim calmly. "That's one of the reasons I'm the right man to go."

WOLFLING

GORDON R. DICKSON

BAEN
science fiction
BOOKS

Copyright © 1968, 1969 by Gordon R. Dickson

A Baen Book

Baen Enterprises
8-10 W. 36th Street
New York, N.Y. 10018

First Baen printing, May 1985

ISBN: 0-671-55962-1

Cover art by Tom Kidd

Printed in the United States of America

Distributed by
SIMON & SCHUSTER
MASS MERCHANDISE SALES COMPANY
1230 Avenue of the Americas
New York, N.Y. 10020

Chapter 1

The bull would not charge.

James Keil stamped his foot and shouted at the animal, but still it would not charge—and it was programmed to charge. Or rather, it was programmed to still be willing to charge at this point in the bullfight.

There was nothing to be done about it. The finest physical tests available could not measure the probable endurance, or bravery, of a bull. This one was tired. Jim would have to step up the pattern and make the kill, now.

He moved toward the bull, stamped and shouted again, and tempted the weary beast into one more attack. As the near horn swept by, grazing his hip and waist, he sucked his belly in hard, feeling a little streak of internal coldness along the line of the graze. Like the bull, he was programmed; and as long as they both stuck to their programming, he was safe. But he was a bullfighter only by courtesy of six months of intensive training. Also, he had free will, where the bull had not—and free will meant the power to break programming and make mistakes.

If he made a mistake, this bull could still kill him.

Therefore he was careful to make no mistakes, even now. The bull was almost at the end of its strength. He led it carefully through a few more passes, then took his sword and went in over the horns for the kill.

The bull grunted, went to its knees, and rolled over on its side as he withdrew the blade. As he watched its death with an impassive face, a female figure appeared without warning on the sand of the arena beside him, looking down at the fallen bull.

He turned to face her. It was the Princess Afuan, aunt of the All-Emperor and head of the visiting party of Highborn who had occupied the official box across the arena, surrounded there by the short, brown-skinned local humans of Alpha Centauri III. Afuan was neither short nor brown—no more than she was, in height or color, in any way similar to an Earth-born Caucasian like Jim himself.

She was dressed—if that was the word—in some sort of white, filmy, cloudstuff. It left her arms bare but covered her otherwise, from the armpits to the ankles, dividing only with the movement of her legs as she walked. Above that cloudstuff, her skin also was white, but not in the sense that Jim's skin was "white."

Afuan's skin was the color of white onyx, and Jim could see the blue veins pulsing dimly within the marble column of her throat. Her face was narrow, and her eyes were large and a startling lemon yellow in color. So that, even though they lacked any epicanthic fold similar to the Oriental, they gave the impression of being slitted and feline below the whitish eyelashes and eyebrows on either side of her long, straight nose. In a sculptured, abstract way, she could have been called beautiful—and she was as tall as Jim himself, who stood six-feet-six.

"Very entertaining," she said now to Jim, speaking the Empire tongue with a rapid, almost hissing accent. "Yes, we'll certainly take you with us, ah—what's your world name, Wolfing?"

"Earthman, High-born," Jim answered

"Yes, well—come to our ship, Earthman. The Throne World will appreciate seeing you," she said. She glanced past him at the other members of his cuadrilla. "But not these others, these assistants of yours; no point in cluttering up the ship. We can supply you anything you need to perform, once you get to the Throne World."

She started to turn away, but Jim spoke.

"Excuse me, High-born," he said. "You can supply me with new assistants; but you can't supply me with the fighting bulls. They've been genetically selected over generations. I've got half a dozen more in cryogenic storage with me here. I'd like to take those."

She turned back to look at him. Her face

was completely unreadable. For a moment Jim was not sure but that in speaking up he had angered her, to the point where she would destroy the work of five years by saying she would not take him along to the Throne World after all. But then she spoke.

"Very well," she said. "Tell whoever takes you aboard our ship that you need these animals shipped too, and that I said they should be."

She turned away again, then, finally, and stood gazing down with interest at the dead bull. As if her movement was a cue, suddenly a dozen or more members of her retinue had also winked into existence on the sand of the arena and were examining the bull and even the suits and equipment of other members of the cuadrilla. The women were none of them more than an inch or two shorter than Afuan; and the tall, slim, onyx-skinned men ranged between six-feet-ten and seven feet in height. Unlike the High-born women, the men wore short kilts and tunics made out of some material more like ordinary cloth. But in almost all cases the color of their clothing was white, except for a single design in some other color, written on either the front or the back of their tunics.

No one offered to examine Jim, as they were examining the others of the cuadrilla. He turned and walked away, sheathing his sword, across the sand and down under the seats of the arena, along a sloping concrete-like passageway illuminated by some source of light apparently within the very material of the walls themselves—one of the Empire luxuries which the local humans of Alpha Centauri III seemed to use without making any effort to understand their workings.

He reached the door of his room, opened it, and stepped inside. Within the windowless main dressing room he saw two things in a single glance.

One was Max Holland, the man from the U.N. Special Committee Section. The other was his own two suitcases, already packed in hopes of the trip to the Throne World, which had now become a reality. But now the suitcases were opened and their contents had been strewn about on the furniture of the room.

"What's this?" Jim said, stopping and looking down at the smaller man. Holland's face was dark with anger.

"Don't think—" he began in a choked voice, and then got control of himself. His voice firmed. "Just because Afuan's agreed to take you doesn't mean you're going to take some of these things to the Throne World!"

"So, you know I'm invited?" Jim asked.

"I'm a good lip-reader," answered Max thickly, "and I had binoculars on you from the moment you started your bullfight until you walked away, just now."

"And you came ahead of me down here and decided to have a look at my luggage?" said Jim.

"That's right!" said Max. He turned sharply and snatched up two items from the couch beside him. One was a Scottish kilt in the Black Watch tartan, with a small knife in a sheath attached to it. The other was a suntan shirt with shoulder tabs, through one of which ran the shoulder belt of a Sam Browne belt, to which was fitted a holster containing a forty-five caliber revolver. Max all but shook these two articles under Jim's nose.

"You're going into the Throne World of a human Empire a hundred thousand years old! A world where they outgrew primitive weapons like this so long ago they probably don't even remember them."

"That's just the point in taking them," said Jim.

He took back the kilt with its small knife and the shirt with its Sam Browne belt from Max's hands so smoothly that the other for a second did not seem to know that they were gone. Jim carried both items of clothing back over to the open suitcases, where he laid them down. He began calmly to repack the luggage.

"*What* point?" Max blazed behind him. "Jim, somehow you seem to have got the idea that you're a loner in this whole project! Just let me remind you—it took a hundred and sixty-two governments, a couple of billion dollars, and the work of thousands of people to train you and bring you here, to the point where you could get yourself invited to play bullfighter on the Throne World!"

Jim, without answering, folded the kilt and placed it back into one of the open suitcases.

"Listen to me, damn you!" snarled Max behind him. The smaller man grabbed Jim's arm and tried to swing him around. Jim turned.

"I'll tell you—*you're not going to take those things!*" said Max.

"Yes, I am," said Jim.

"I say you're not!" shouted Max. "Who do you think you are, anyway? You're just the man who was picked to go into the Throne World and observe. Got that? *Observe!* Not stick people with knives, or shoot them with guns, or do anything else to draw any more Imperial attention to Earth than there is already. You're an anthropologist, play-acting a bullfighter, not some cloak-and-dagger spy!"

"I'm all three," said Jim quickly and a little coldly.

The color slowly went from Max's face. "God . . ." said the smaller man. His hand fell away from Jim's arm. "Ten years ago we didn't know they existed—a whole empire of human-occupied worlds stretching in from Alpha Centauri here toward the galactic center. Five years ago you were only a name on a list. I could have put a pencil mark through you, and you wouldn't have been here now. Even a year ago I was ready to start questioning whether we'd been training the right man—and you picked just then to put on such a good show nobody'd have listened to me. Now it turns out I was right, after all. An Empire of a thousand worlds, and one little Earth. They forgot us once, and maybe they could forget us again—but not if you're the man who goes in and observes them. I was right a year ago. You've got some ax of your own to grind with these High-born—"

He choked and broke off. He breathed deeply and straightened his back.

"Forget it," he said more calmly. "You're not going. I'm aborting the project—on my own responsibility. Earth can ask me all the questions they want, after that Imperial ship leaves—"

"Max," said Jim almost gently. "It's too late for you to stop me now. I've been invited by the Princess Afuan. Not you, or the whole project, or the whole Earth would be let interfere with her invitation now. Do you think she'd allow that?"

Max stood staring at Jim with dark-circled, bloodshot eyes. He did not answer.

"I'm sorry, Max," said Jim. "But it was bound to come to this sooner or later. From here on out the project can't guide me any longer. From now on I have to follow my own judgment."

He turned back to his packing.

"*Your* judgment!" A little moisture flew with the words, to touch coldly against the side and back of Jim's neck. "You're so sure of your judgment? Compared to those Highborn like Afuan, you're just as ignorant, just as primitive, just as savage as all the rest of us back on Earth! You don't know anything! Maybe Earth *is* one of their colonies that they forgot about.... Or maybe it's just coincidence that we seem to belong to the same race as them and these people we found her on Alpha Centauri III! Who knows? I don't; no Earthman does. And neither do you! So don't talk about your judgment to me, Jim! Not with the whole future of Earth riding on what you do, once you get there, into the Imperial household!"

Jim shrugged. He turned back to his packing and felt his arm violently seized and wrenched as Max tried to turn him around once more.

Swiftly, this time, Jim turned. He knocked Max's grip loose with the edge of his right hand, and then put that same hand, calmingly, it seemed, upon the smaller man's shoulder. But the thumb reached up from the grip of the other four fingers to lay itself against Max's neck behind the right point of the angle of his jawbone; and it pressed in slightly.

Max's face whitened, and he gasped. He drew a quick, short breath and tried to back away. But the grip of Jim's hand held him.

"You—you're a fool!" stammered Max. "You'd *kill* me?"

"If I had to," said Jim calmly. "That's one of the reasons I'm the right man to go."

He released his grip, turned away, closed the open suitcase into which he had put the kilt and the shirt with the Sam Browne belt, and picked up both the heavy suitcases. He turned and went out through the door, turning left and away up the corridor in the opposite direction, which led to the street and the vehicle that was waiting for him outside the arena. As he neared the entrance, he heard Max shouting after him, his words distorted by the long tunnel of the corridor. Glancing back, he saw that the other man had come out of the dressing room to stand staring after him.

"Observe!" Max shouted in English after him up the corridor. "Do anything else, Jim, get Earth into trouble with the High-born, and we'll shoot you for it, like a mad dog, when you get home again!"

Jim did not answer. He stepped out into the bright, yellow sunlight of Alpha Centauri III, and into the open, four-wheeled, jeeplike vehicle that was there waiting for him with its driver at the controls.

Chapter 2

The driver of the vehicle was a staff member of the Earth Trade Delegation, which, with the trade delegations from two other Empire-inhabited solar systems, had combined with the Alpha Centaurans of this planet to put on various local-culture shows for the visiting High-born. It was always the hope of those putting on such shows that the result would be some form of preference by the High-born visitors. Earth had stood the best chance of arousing interest, being, in theory, a newly rediscovered part of the Empire, and now its show of the art of bullfighting was being carried back by the visitors to the Throne World to amuse the Emperor.

The driver took Jim and his luggage through the surrounding city and out to the open spaceport, an endless stretch of brownish, cementlike material. In one area of this, all by itself, sat a huge ovoid that was the ship of the High-born. The driver drove Jim up to this ship and stopped.

"Want me to wait?" asked the driver.

Jim shook his head. He took the two suit-cases out of the vehicle and watched as the driver put it in motion and drove off, dwindling to toy size in the distance across the spaceport area.

Jim set his suitcases down and turned to look at the ship. From the outside it seemed perfectly featureless. There were no ports, no airlocks, no signs of apertures or entrances to the interior. Nor did anyone aboard the huge vessel seem to be aware that Jim was there.

He sat down on one of his suitcases and began to wait.

For a little over an hour nothing happened. Then, abruptly, while he was still sitting on his suitcase, he was no longer on the space-port concrete, but with both bags in what appeared to be a green-walled, egg-shaped room with some sort of darker green carpet underfoot and cushions of all colors and sizes, from six inches in diameter to something like six feet, furnishing it

"Were you waiting long, Wolfling?" asked a girl's voice. "I'm sorry. I was busy taking care of the other pets."

He stood up and turned about from his suitcase; and he saw her then. By the standards of the High-born, she was short—probably no more than five feet, ten inches in height. Also her skin, although it approached the onyx-white of the Princess Afuan and the others, had a brownish tinge, like a pale shadow of the brownishness of an American Indian. The brownishness extended to her eyes, which were rather a dark gold, flecked with little sparkles of red highlights—not like the lemon yellow Jim had seen in Afuan. Her face was less long than Afuan's, and more rounded of jaw. She smiled in a way that was very unlike the inscrutability of the High-born princess; and when she smiled, the ghosts of a small cloud of something like freckles appeared across her nose and up her cheeks. Finally, her hair, though she let it hang straight down her back, as had the other High-born females Jim had seen in the arena, was plainly yellow-blond rather than white, and it did not hang as straight as Afuan's, but had a perceptible wave and thickness to it.

Her smile vanished and her face darkened suddenly with an abrupt flood of blood below the skin. It was a literal flush—the last thing Jim had expected to discover upon the face of one of the High-born.

"That's right, stare at me!" she said spiritedly. "I'm not ashamed of it!"

"Ashamed of what?" asked Jim.

"Why—" She broke off suddenly. Her blush fled, and she looked at him contritely. "I'm sorry. Of course—you're a Wolfling. You wouldn't even know the difference, would you?"

"Evidently not," said Jim. "Because I don't seem to understand what you're talking about."

She laughed—but a little sadly, it seemed

to him; and patted his arm unexpectedly, with a light, consoling touch.

"You'll learn soon enough," she said, "even if you are a Wolfling. I'm a throwback, you see. Something in my gene pattern was atavistic. Oh, my father and mother were as High-born as anyone outside the Main Royal Line; and Afuan will never dismiss me from her household. But, on the other hand, she can hardly show me off. So I'm left with doing things like taking care of the pets for her. That was why I was the one who brought you on board just now."

She glanced down at his two cases.

"Is that your equipment there?" she asked. "I'll put it away for you."

Instantly the two pieces of luggage vanished.

"Just a minute," said Jim.

She looked up at him, a little puzzled.

"Didn't you want them put away just yet?" she asked. Instantly the bags were back at their feet.

"No," answered Jim. "It's just that there are other things to bring aboard. I told your Princess Afuan that I'd need the bulls—the creatures I work with when I put on my show. I've got six more of them in cryogenic storage back in the city. She said I could bring them along, and to tell whoever brought me aboard the ship that she said it was all right."

"Oh!" said the girl thoughtfully. "No—

don't try to tell me. Just think about where
they are in the city."

Jim obliged by summoning up a mental
picture of the refrigerated warehouse behind the compound housing the Earth Trade
Delegation, where his bulls were stored. He
felt a curious light touch in his mind—a
sort of passing sensation, as if his naked
brain had been lightly brushed by a feather.
Abruptly he and the girl were standing in
the refrigerated warehouse, before the stack
of six huge cases, each with the frozen body
of a fighting bull in suspended animation
within it.

"—Yes," said the girl thoughtfully. Abruptly they were someplace else.

This new place was a large, metal-walled
chamber with a small assortment of cases
and other objects arranged in neat piles at
intervals about its floor. The stack of cases
containing the frozen bulls was now here
also. Jim frowned. The temperature of the
room was clearly in the comfortable seventy-
degree range.

"These animals are frozen," he told the
girl. "And they have to stay frozen—"

"Oh, don't worry about that," she interrupted; and then smiled at him, half in
cheerfulness, half, it seemed, in apology for
interrupting him. "Nothing about their condition will change. I've left orders with the
ship's controls to see to that."

Her smile widened.

"Go ahead," she said. "Put your hand out and feel for yourself."

Jim reached out his hand toward the side of the nearest case. There was no change in temperature until his fingertips came within an inch or two of the surface of the case—then they suddenly encountered bone-chilling atmosphere. The cold, he knew, could not come from the cases, since these were superbly insulated. He withdrew his hand.

"I see," he said. "All right. I won't worry about my bulls."

"Good," she answered.

Instantly they were elsewhere. Not back in the egg-shaped room but in another, a long room, one side of which appeared to be glass looking out on a strip of beach and the surf of an ocean shore—the shore of an ocean aboard a spaceship was no less startling than the other things to be seen within the rectangular, glass-walled room itself.

These were a variety of creatures, running from something like a small, purple-furred squirrel to a creature farther down the room who was tall and covered with black fur—more than apelike, but still less than human.

"These are my other pets," he heard the girl saying at his elbow, and looked down into her smiling face. "I mean—they're really Afuan's pets. The ones I take care of for her. This one—"

She stopped to pet the small, purple-furred squirrel, which arched itself like a

satisfied cat under her hand. Neither it nor
any of the others seemed to be chained or
restrained in any way. Yet they all stayed
some little distance from one another.

"—This one," the girl repeated, "is Ifny—"

She stopped suddenly, jumping to her feet.

"I'm sorry, Wolfling," she said. "You must
have a name too. What is it?"

"James Keil," he answered her. "Call me
Jim."

"*Jim*," she echoed, trying it out, with her
head cocked on one side. In her Empire
accent, the '*m*' sound was prolonged, so that
the short, familiar form of James came out
sounding more musical than it might have
in English.

"And your name?" Jim asked her.

She started, and looked at him almost in
shock.

"But you should call me High-born!" she
said a little stiffly. But the next moment the
stiffness had melted, as if her interior warmth
of character would not endure it. "But I do
have a name, of course. I have several doz-
ens of them, in fact. But you know we all go
by one name familiarly. My normally used
name is Ro."

Jim inclined his head.

"Thank you, High-born," he said.

"Oh, call me Ro—" she broke off, as if a
little frightened at what she was saying.
"When we're alone, anyway. After all, you
are human, even if you are a Wolfling, Jim."

"That's something else you can tell me,

then, Ro," said Jim. "What is this 'Wolfling' that everyone calls me?"

She stared at him for a moment, almost blankly.

"But you—no, of course, you'd be the very one who wouldn't know!" she said. Once more she blushed in that remarkable fashion he had noticed earlier. Plainly it was the lightness of her skin, for all its brown tint, that caused the sudden rush of blood to her features to be seen. But it was unusual to Jim to see such a marked reaction in any adult woman. "It's ... not a very nice name for you, I'm afraid. It means— it means something like ... you're a human being, all right, but one who's been lost in the woods and brought up by animals, so that you don't have any idea of what it's really like to be a human."

Her blush flared again.

"I'm sorry ..." she said, looking down. "I shouldn't have called you that myself. But I didn't think. I'll always call you Jim, from now on."

Jim smiled. "It doesn't matter," he said.

"Yes, it does!" she said fiercely, looking up at him abruptly. "I know what it's like to be called names. I never let anybody call any of my—Afuan's—pets names. And I'm not going to let anybody call you names if I can help it."

"Well, thank you, then," said Jim gently. She patted his arm again soothingly.

"Come meet my other pets," she said, moving down the line.

He went with her. The creatures in the room seemed free to wander about the room, but at the same time enclosed and protected by an invisible barrier that kept them from coming any closer than four or five feet to one of the other creatures. They were plainly all animals. Curiously, also, they all appeared to resemble, at least to some extent, an animal type that either was on Earth or had been at some period in its geologic history. This, in itself, was interesting. It seemed to substantiate the Empire's assumption that the people of Earth were part of its own basic stock—lost, only to be found again when they ventured by their own scientific powers back in as far as Alpha Centauri. The alternative was to assume that human-habitable planets had evolutionary parallels to an extremely remarkable degree.

Still, even this could be; a parallelism among fauna on various worlds did not absolutely prove a common ancestry for its dominant species.

Jim noticed something also that was very interesting about Ro herself. Most of the animals responded happily when she spoke to them or petted them. Even those who did not—and she handled even the fiercest of them without hesitation—showed absolutely no hostility. The farthest they got from expressions of happiness at her attention was something like a lazy indifference.

Such as in the case of one large catlike creature—easily as big as a South American jaguar and somewhat resembling the jaguar in its spotted coat, although a heavy, horselike head spoiled the general picture. This catlike creature yawned and allowed itself to be petted but made no great effort to respond to Ro's caresses. The apelike creature in the black hair, in contrast, sadly clung to her hand and gazed into her face as she spoke to it and stroked its head; but it made no other response

Letting go of its hand at last—pulling away, in fact—Ro turned finally to Jim.

"Now you've seen them," she said. "Maybe you'll help me take care of them sometimes. They really should have more attention than I give them alone. Afuan forgets she has them for months on end. . . . Oh, that won't happen to you—" She interrupted herself suddenly. "You understand? You're to perform for the Emperor when we get back to the Throne World. And as I say, you're not an animal."

"Thank you," said Jim gravely.

She looked surprised, then laughed. She patted his arm in the gesture he was beginning to find customary on her part.

"Now," she said, "you'll want to get to your own quarters."

Instantly they were in a room that they had not been in before. Like the room containing the pets, it had a glass wall window looking out on the beach and the ocean beyond, which, whether illusion or reality, rolled its surf within thirty feet of the glass wall itself.

"These will be your quarters," said Ro. Jim looked around him. There was no sign of a door in any of the walls.

"Don't you suppose," he said, "you'd better tell this Wolfling how to get around from one room to the next?"

"To the next?" she echoed with a puzzled frown, and suddenly he realized that she had taken him literally. His mind seized on the implications of that.

"I'm sorry," he said; "I simply meant from this room to any other room. But—just for the fun of it—what is the room that's just beyond that wall there?"

He pointed to the blank wall of the room opposite the one of glass overlooking the beach and the ocean.

She stared at the wall, frowned again, and finally shook her head.

"Why . . . I don't know," she said. "But what difference does it make? You go to all rooms the same way. So there's really no difference. It doesn't matter where in the ship they are."

Jim filed this information mentally for future reference. "I should know how to get myself from room to room, though, shouldn't I?" he asked.

"Oh," she said, "I'm sorry. Of course, you don't know. The ship runs everything. You have to tune in to the ship; then it'll do anything you want."

She lit up suddenly.

"Would you like to see what the rest of the ship looks like?" she asked. "I'll take you around. Why don't you get yourself settled in here, or unpack, or whatever you want to do; and I'll come back in a little while. How soon should I come back?"

Jim mentioned a time in Empire units that was roughly the equivalent of fifteen minutes.

"Fine," Ro said, smiling at him. "I'll be right back when the time's up."

She vanished.

Left alone, Jim examined the room, which was furnished with hassocks and pillows of all size—much as the first room he had seen aboard ship, where he had met Ro. The one very large hassock, some four feet thick and eight feet in diameter, at one end of the room, he took to be the bed. At first there seemed nothing in the shape of a bathroom. But the moment this thought occurred to him a section of the wall obediently slid aside, and he found himself looking into a smaller room fitted out with a complete assortment of recognizable lavatory facilities, up to and including a swimming pool—and with several other articles of plumbing which seemed to make little sense. For example, there was one shallow, completely dry basin large enough for him to stretch out in.

He turned back to his main room and with a corner of his eye saw the door to the bathroom slide shut behind him. He picked up his two suitcases, put them on the bedlike hassock, and opened them. No sooner had he done so than another section of the wall opened, and he found himself looking into what might have been the closet if there had been any pole or clothes hangers in it.

Experimentally—he was beginning to get the hang of things aboard ship now—he tried to imagine his clothes as being hung up in the closet.

Obligingly, they were suddenly there—the only unusual part of their appearance and situation being that they hung as he had imagined them, but without any visible means of support, suspended vertically in midair as if held by invisible hangers from an invisible rod.

Jim nodded. He was about to think the closet closed again, when a second thought made him take the Scottish costume, complete with kilt and knife, from where it hung unsupported in midair, and change into it, placing his suit of lights in the closet in its place, where it hung invisibly supported with the rest of his clothes.

The closet closed, and Jim was just turning away from it when a visitor materialized in the center of his room. But it was not Ro. Instead, it was one of the male High-born—a man with onyx-white skin, at least seven feet tall.

"There you are, Wolfling," the High-born said. "Come along. Mekon wants to see you."

They were suddenly in a room which Jim had not been in before. It was rectangular and long, and they stood in about the middle of it. There were no other humans in the room. But at the far end, on a sort of pillow-strewn dais, there lay curled a feline similar in every respect to the one among Ro's pets. It lifted its horse's head at the sight of them in the room, and its eyes fastened upon Jim.

"Wait here," said the High-born who had brought him. "Mekon will be with you in just a moment."

The tall man vanished. Jim found himself left alone with the feline beast, which was now lazily rising to its feet, staring down the room at him.

Jim stood still, staring back.

The animal made a curious, whining sound—a sound almost ridiculously small to come from something obviously so physically powerful. Its short stub of a tufted tail began to jerk vertically up and down, stiffly. Its heavy head lowered until its lower jaw almost touched the floor of the dias, and its mouth gradually opened to reveal heavy, carnivorous teeth.

Still whining, it began slowly to move. Softly, almost delicately, it put one front paw down from the dais; and then the other. Slowly it began to move toward him, crouching and whining as it did. Its teeth were fully visible now, and as it approached, its whine grew in volume, until it was a sort of singing threat.

Jim waited, moving neither backward nor forward.

The animal came on. About a dozen yards from him it stopped and gradually crouched. Its tail was jerking like a metronome now, and the singing whine that came from its throat was filling the whole room.

For what seemed a long time, it crouched there, jaw hung open, whining. Then, without warning, the whining stopped, and it launched itself through the air at Jim's throat.

Chapter 3

The feline creature flashed forward and upward into Jim's face—and vanished

Jim had not moved. For a moment he
was alone in the long, rectangular room;
and then suddenly there were three of the
High-born males around him, one of them
with the dragonlike insignia upon his shirt,
or tunic, front. That one had brought Jim
here. Of the other two, one was almost short
by High-born standards-barely three inches
taller than Jim. The third was the tallest of
the three—a slim, rather graceful-looking
man with the first expression resembling a
smile Jim had ever seen on purely onyx-
colored features; and this last of the three
High-born wore a red insignia which looked
somewhat like the horns and head of a stag.

"I told you they were brave, these Wolflings," drawled this last member of the
group. "Your trick didn't work, Mekon."

"*Courage!*" said the one addressed as
Mekon angrily. "That was too good to be
true. He didn't even move a muscle! You'd
think he'd been—" Mekon bit off the words

abruptly, glancing hastily at the tall Slothiel, who stiffened.

"Go on. Go on, Mekon," drawled the tall High-born, but there was an edge to his drawl now. "You were going to say something like . . . 'warned'?"

"Of course Mekon didn't mean to say anything like that." It was Trahey, almost literally pushing himself between the other two men, whose eyes were now fixedly fastened on each other.

"I'd like to hear Mekon tell me that," murmured Slothiel.

Mekon's eyes dropped. "I—of course, I didn't mean anything of the sort. I don't remember what I was going to say," he said.

"Then I take it," said Slothiel, "that I've won. One Lifetime Point, to me?"

"One—" The admission clearly stuck in Mekon's throat. His face had darkened with a rush of blood similar to the flush that Jim had noticed come too easily to the face of Ro. "One Lifetime Point to you."

Slothiel laughed. "Don't take it so hard, man," he said. "You can have a chance to win it back anytime you've got a decent wager to propose."

But Mekon's temper had flared again. "All right," he snapped, and swung to face Jim. "I've given up the point—but I'd still like to know why this Wolfling didn't even twitch when the beast went for him. There's something unnatural here."

"Why don't you ask him?" drawled Slothiel.

"I *am* asking him!" said Mekon, his eyes burning upon Jim. "Speak up, Wolfling. Why didn't you show any sign of a reaction?"

"The Princess Afuan is taking me to the Throne World to show me off to the Emperor," Jim answered quietly. "I could hardly be shown off if I were badly torn up or killed by an animal like that one. Therefore, whoever was responsible for the cat coming at me was certain to make sure that I wouldn't be hurt by it."

Slothiel threw back his head and laughed loudly. Mekon's face, which had paled back to its normal color, now flushed again with a dark rush of angry blood

"So!" snapped Mekon. "You think you can't be touched, is that it, Wolfling? I'll show you—"

He broke off, for Ro had suddenly appeared in the room beside them; and now she literally shoved herself between Jim and the angry High-born.

"What're you doing to him?" she cried. "He's supposed to be left with me! He's not for the rest of you to play with—"

"Why, you little mud-skinned throwback!" snapped Mekon. His hand darted out to the small black stick running through the two loops of the ropelike material that acted as a belt to her white dress. "Give me that rod!"

As his hand closed upon it, she snatched

at it herself; and for a moment there was a
tug-of-war in which the rod had come loose
from the belt and they both had hold of it.

"Let go, you little—" Mekon raised one
hand, clenching his fingers into a fist as
though to strike down at Ro; and, at that
moment, Jim stepped suddenly up to him.

The High-born yelled suddenly—it was
almost a bass scream—and let go of the
rod, falling back and holding his right arm
with his left hand. All down along his forearm a line dripped red, and Jim was putting the little knife back into its scabbard.

There was a sudden, utter, frozen silence
in the room. Trahey, the heretofore self-
possessed Slothiel, and even Ro were ut-
terly still, staring at the blood running down
Mekon's forearm. If the walls of the ship
had begun to crumble about them, they
could not have looked more overwhelmed
and stupefied.

"He—the Wolfling damaged me," stuttered
Mekon, staring wildly at his bleeding arm.
"Did you see what he did?"

Slowly Mekon raised his eyes to his two
companions.

"Did you see what he did?" Mekon screamed. "Get me a rod! Don't just stand there!
Get me a rod!"

Trahey made a slow move as if to step
toward Ro, but Slothiel, with suddenly nar-
rowed eyes, caught Trahey's arm.

"No, no," murmured Slothiel. "Our little

game isn't a game anymore. If he wants rods, let him get them himself."

Trahey stood still. Ro abruptly disappeared.

"Blind you, Trahey!" shouted Mekon. "I'll collect from you for this! Get me a rod, I say!"

Trahey slowly shook his head, though his lips were almost bloodless.

"A rod—no No, Mekon," he said. "Slothiel's right. You'll have to do that for yourself."

"Then I will!" screamed Mekon—and disappeared.

"I still say you're a brave man, Wolfling," said Slothiel to Jim. "Let me give you a piece of advice. If Mekon offers you a rod, don't take it."

Trahey made an odd little sound, like a man who has started to speak and then suddenly thought better of it. Slothiel turned his eyes upon the other High-born.

"You were going to say something, Trahey?" he asked. "Perhaps you were going to object to my advising the Wolfling?"

Trahey shook his head. But the glance he threw at Jim was baleful.

Mekon suddenly reappeared, his arm still bleeding, but the hand at the end of it clutching two short black rods like the one Ro had worn in the loops of her belt. He held one of these in his good hand, and stepping forward, thrust it at Jim.

"Take this, Wolfling!" he snapped.

Jim shook his head and drew the small knife from his kilt.

"No thanks," he said. "I think I'll stick to this."

Mekon's face lit up savagely

"Suit yourself!" he said, and threw the rod he had offered across the room. "It makes no difference to me—"

"But it does to me!" cut in a new voice. It was a woman's voice, behind Jim. Jim turned quickly and backed off a step so as to keep everyone in the room in front of him. Ro had reappeared, he saw; and with her was a tall female High-born whom Jim believed he recognized as Afuan. Behind both women towered a slim High-born male, possibly even an inch or two taller than Slothiel.

"Well?" went on Afuan, if it was indeed she. "Has something happened to alter the tables of precedence, so that you think you can take it on yourself to rod one of my pets, Mekon?"

Mekon had frozen. Even the expression on his face, caught halfway between rage and astonishment, seemed fixed there by a sort of paralysis.

Behind the two women the unusually tall male High-born smiled slowly. It was a smile something like the lazy smile of Slothiel, but there was more of a feeling of power— and perhaps more of cruelty—in it.

"I'm afraid you've offended Her Majesty, Mekon," he said. "That could cost you more than a few Lifetime Points. Men have been banished to the Colony Worlds for less."

Surprisingly, it was Slothiel who came to the defense of the paralyzed Mekon.

"Not perhaps in just such a case as this," said Slothiel. "The Wolfling assaulted Mekon first. Certainly someone like Galyan would understand how a man could react to something like that."

The eyes of the tall High-born addressed as Galyan went out to meet with Slothiel's. They looked at each other with a mutual amusement that seemed to hang upon the very lip of animosity. *Someday*, those looks seemed to say, *we will clash, but not now.* The Princess Afuan noticed the exchange, and instantly her own manner changed to one of brisk reasonableness.

"Nonsense!" she said. "He's only a Wolfling, after all!— Do you enjoy looking disgusting, man?" This last phrase was addressed to Mekon. "Heal yourself!"

Mekon woke abruptly from his trance and looked down at his wounded arm. Jim looked at it also; and before his eyes he saw the long shallow cut slowly begin to close and firm over—without any of the ordinary signs of scabbing or healing. Within perhaps a second and a half the wound had disappeared, leaving only white-onyx skin that looked as if it had never been cut. The dried blood on the arm remained, but after a second Mekon passed his other hand along it, and this too vanished. He was left with an arm not only whole but clean. Jim put the knife back into its scabbard at his belt.

"That's better," said Afuan. She turned to the tall man beside her. "I'll leave it to you now, Galyan. See that Mekon pays some kind of a fine."

She vanished.

"You can go too, girl," Galyan said, looking down at Ro. "I didn't have a chance to watch this Wolfling putting on his act on the planet. After I deal with Mekon, I'd like to examine the wild man myself."

Ro hesitated. Her face was unhappy

"Go along," said Galyan softly but sharply. "I'm not going to hurt your Wolfling! You'll have him back in perfect shape before you know it."

Ro hesitated a second longer, then vanished, in her turn, casting a strangely appealing glance at Jim just before she went, as if to caution him against any act that might lead to further trouble.

"Come with me, Wolfling," said Galyan. He disappeared. After a second, he reappeared, smiling quizzically at Jim.

"So you don't know how to move around in the ship, do you?" he said. "Very well, Wolfling. I'll provide your motive power."

At once Jim found himself in a large, oval, low-ceilinged room with yellow walls, which more resembled an office or a place of work than any of the rooms he had so far visited aboard the vessel. At hard-surfaced slabs of what looked like stone floating in midair and plainly in use as desktops, three men were at work—none of them High-born.

Two were brown, squat men—about the color of a white-skinned human from Earth with a good heavy suntan. They were no more than five and a half feet tall. The third, who was looking at what appeared to be a map, was possibly six inches taller and a hundred pounds heavier than the other two. His greater weight was not in body fat, but plainly in a very heavy, even massive skeleton and corresponding musculature. Unlike the two shorter men, who had long, straight brown hair hanging down their backs almost in the fashion in which the white hair of the High-born women was allowed to hang, the third man was completely bald. His round, hairless skull, with its grayish skin stretched tightly over the bone beneath, was the most prominent feature about him, so that it made his eyes, his nose, his mouth, and even his fairly good-sized ears seem small by comparison. This third man got up on seeing Galyan and Jim appear in the room.

"No, no. It's all right, Reas," said Galyan. "Back to your work."

The powerful-looking man sat down again without a word and returned to his map study.

"Reas," said Galyan, waving a hand at him, and looking down at Jim, "is what you might call my bodyguard. Although I don't need a bodyguard—no more than any of the High-born do. Does that surprise you?"

"I don't know enough about it to be ei-

ther surprised or not surprised," answered
Jim.

Galyan nodded, surprisingly, as if in approval.

"No, of course you don't," he said. He sat
down on a handy cushion and reached out
a long arm.

"Let me see that tool of yours," he said.
"The one you used to hurt Mekon."

Jim drew the knife and passed it over,
hilt first. Galyan accepted it gingerly, holding it between a thumb and two opposing
fingers. He held it up in the air before his
eyes and tenderly touched its point and edges
with the long forefinger of his left hand.
Then he handed it back to Jim.

"I suppose you could kill an ordinary man
with something like that," he said.

"Yes," said Jim.

"Very interesting," said Galyan. He sat
for a moment, as if caught up in his own
thoughts. Then his eyes focused on Jim once
more. "You realize, I suppose, that you aren't
allowed to go around damaging the High-
born with tools like that?"

Jim said nothing. In the face of his silence,
Galyan smiled, almost as he had smiled
at Slothiel—a little enigmatically, a little
cruelly.

"You're very interesting, Wolfling," he said
slowly. "Very interesting indeed. You don't
seem to realize that you exist like an insect
in the palm of any one of us who are High-
born. Now, someone like Mekon would have

closed his hand and crushed the life out of you long before this. In fact, that is just what he was about to do when Afuan and I stopped him. But I'm not the sort of High-born that Mekon is. In fact, I am like no other High-born you will meet—except the Emperor; and, since we're first cousins, that's not surprising. So I'm not going to close my hand on you, Wolfling. I'm going to reason with you—as if you were High-born yourself."

"Thank you," said Jim.

"You do not thank me, Wolfling," said Galyan softly. "You do not thank me, or curse me, or plead with me, or praise me. You do nothing where I am concerned—but listen. And answer when you are questioned. Now, to begin with. How did you get into that room with Mekon, Trahey, and Slothiel?"

Jim told him briefly and emotionlessly.

"I see," said Galyan. He clasped his long hands around one knee and leaned back a little on his cushion, looking at a slight slant up into Jim's face. "So you trusted to the fact that the Princess intended to show you off to the Emperor, and that for that reason no one else would dare harm you. Even if such a faith were justified, Wolfling, you showed a rather remarkable control of your nerves to stand absolutely still while that beast jumped at your face."

He paused, as if to give Jim a chance to say something. When Jim did not, he mur-

mured, almost deprecatingly, "You have my
leave to speak."

"What would you like me to speak about?"
asked Jim.

Galyan's lemon-yellow eyes glowed almost
like a cat's eyes in the dark.

"Yes," he murmured, drawing the *s* sound
out slowly, "you are most unusual—even
for a Wolfling. Though I haven't actually
met that many Wolflings, so that I don't
consider myself much of a judge. You're
fairly good-sized for someone not High-born.
Tell me, the rest of your people aren't as
big as you, are they?"

"On the average, no," said Jim.

"Then there're bigger males among you?"

"Yes," said Jim, without expanding on
the subject.

"As large as the High-born?" asked Galyan.
"Are there any as tall as myself?"

"Yes," said Jim.

"But not many," said Galyan, his eyes
glowing. "In fact, they're rare. Isn't that
so?"

"That's right," said Jim.

"In fact," said Galyan, nursing his knee,
"to be truthful about it, you might say that
they are practically in the case of freaks—
aren't they?"

"You might say that," said Jim.

"Yes, I thought we'd get at the truth,"
said Galyan. "You see, Wolfling, we of the
High-born are not freaks. We're a true
aristocracy—an aristocracy of not merely

inherited power superior to anything else
owned by the various races of man. We're
superior physically, mentally, and emotionally. This is a fact that you will not have
grasped yet; and normally the practice
would have been to let you discover it the
hard way on your own. However, I've taken
an interest in you. . . ."

He turned to Reas.

"Bring me a couple of rods," he said.

The heavy-boned bodyguard got up from
his map, went across the room, and came
back holding a pair of short black rods like
the one Jim had seen at Ro's belt and like
the two which Mekon had produced after
Jim had used the knife on him. Another
black rod, just like the two in Reas' hands,
Jim noticed, was stuck through loops in the
ropelike belt that encircled Reas' thick waist.

"Thank you, Reas," said Galyan, accepting the two rods. He turned to Jim. "I told
you that you won't find other High-born
like me. I'm remarkably free of prejudice
toward the lesser races of man—not out of
any sentimentality, but out of practicality.
But I would like to show you something."

He turned his head and beckoned to one
of the small, brown-skinned men with the
brown hair hanging straight down his back.
The man got up and came over to stand
beside Reas, and Galyan handed him one of
the two black rods. The man stuck it through
the belt around his own waist.

"Reas, as I said," said Galyan to Jim, "is

not only trained but actually bred to be a bodyguard. Now, observe how he handles his rod, compared to his opponent here."

Galyan turned to Reas and the other man, who were now facing each other at a distance of about four feet.

"I will clap my hands twice," said Galyan to them. "The first clap commences the draw— only, Reas will not be allowed to draw until the second clap. Observe, Wolfling!"

Galyan lifted his hands and clapped them softly together twice, the second clap following about a half-second behind the first. At the sound of the first clap, the small brown man snatched the rod from his belt and was just bringing its far end up to point at Reas when the second clap sounded and Reas drew his own rod swiftly and smoothly.

Just then, something in appearance like a cross between the flame of a welding torch and the arc of a static-electricity charge crackled from the end of the rod held by the smaller man. It was aimed directly at the chest of Reas, but it never reached its target. Even as it burst from the end of the rod, Reas' rod was already in position, and a counterdischarge met and deflected the discharge from the smaller man's rod, so that both charges went upward.

"Very good," said Galyan. The discharge from both rods ceased, and both men lowered their rods and turned to face the Highborn. Galyan reached out and took the rod from the small brown man and dismissed him with a wave back to his work.

"Now, watch closely, Wolfling," said Galyan. He slid the black rod he held into a pair of loops on his own belt; and as if in response to an unseen signal, the bodyguard, Reas, did the same with his rod.

"Now, as I say—observe, Wolfling," said Galyan softly. "Reas can draw at any time he wishes."

Reas stepped forward until he was less than an arm's length from the seated Highborn. For a moment he stood completely motionless; then he looked off into a corner of the room; and at the same moment his hand flashed toward his belt.

There was a sudden sharp *click!* Galyan's arm was extended, and the rod in his hand was holding Reas' rod in half-drawn position from its belt loops. Galyan chuckled softly and released the pressure he was putting against the other rod. He handed his rod back to Reas, who took them away across the room.

"You see?" said Galyan, turning to Jim. "Any High-born has faster reflexes than any single human of any of the other races of man. Let alone wild men like yourselves. That was why in going after rods as Mekon did, he was intending to force you into a duel that you had no chance whatsoever of winning. As I say, we are true aristocracy. Not only are my reflexes faster than those of Reas, but my memory is better, my intelligence is greater, my discernment and perceptions are sharper than those of any other human beings—yes, even among the Highborn themselves. But, in spite of that, I employ more of the low-born than any of my fellow High-born. I have many things for them to do, and I keep them busy at it. Do you wonder why I do this, when I myself could do any of these things better, by and for myself?"

"I'd assume," said Jim, "for the simple reason that you can't be in two places at once."

Galyan's eyes glowed with a new intensity.

"What a brilliant Wolfling it is!" he said. "Yes, other men are useful to me, even though they are inferior. And it strikes me, just now, that maybe you and the little tool of yours with which you damaged Mekon might one day be useful to me, too. Are you surprised to hear that?"

"Not after you spent this much time on me," said Jim.

Galyan rocked himself softly on his cushion, holding to his knee.

"Better and better," he murmured. "This Wolfling has a brain—raw gray matter, of course. But a brain, nonetheless. I wasn't wrong. Yes, I may have a use for you, Wolfling—and do you know why you'll be useful to me when the time comes?"

"You must plan to pay me, some way or another," said Jim.

"Exactly," said Galyan. "We High-born

do not show our age, so I'll tell you right now, Wolfling, that while I'm by no means into middle age, as we know lifetimes, still, I'm not a raw youngster anymore. And I've learned how to get members of the lesser human races to work for me. I give them whatever they most want by way of reward and payment."

He paused. Jim waited.

"Well, Wolfling," said Galyan after a minute, "what is it you want most? If you were not a wild man, I wouldn't have to ask you. But I don't know Wolflings well enough to know what they want. What do they want most?"

"Freedom," said Jim.

Galyan smiled.

"Of course," he said. "What all wild beasts want—or think they want. Freedom. And in your case, freedom means the right to come and go, doesn't it?"

"That's the base of it," said Jim.

"Particularly the right to go, I should think," murmured Galyan. "No doubt you never stopped to think of it, Wolfling, but it is simple fact that once you have been taken in by us to the Throne World, you would have no way of ever going back to the place where we first found you. Did you realize that? That, once you joined us on this trip to the Throne World, you would never be able to go home again?"

Jim stared down at him.

"No," he said, "I hadn't planned never to go home again."

"Well, that's your situation," said Galyan. He lifted a slim forefinger. "*Unless* you turn out to be useful to me. I might see to it that you got home again."

He let go of his knee and rose suddenly to his feet, towering over Jim.

"I'll send you back to Ro now," he said. "Carry that thought I've just given you away with you. Your only hope of ever seeing the world from which you came again is if in some way you please me."

The High-born made no further movement, but abruptly Jim found himself back in the glass-walled room with the other pets. Ro was crouched at one end, weeping over the body of one of the feline creatures. It was not the one who had been among the pets, because this one now stood, whining anxiously, just out of reach of the tearful girl. It was another one that lay dead—and it looked rather as if it had been cut almost in half by a thunderbolt.

Chapter 4

Jim went to the girl. She was not aware of his presence until he had reached down and put his arms around her. She looked up, startled and suddenly stiff; but then, when she saw who it was, she clung to him.

"You're all right. At least, you're all right . . ." she managed to get out.

"Where did this come from?" asked Jim, pointing down at the dead feline.

The question triggered off a new burst of emotion. But gradually the story began to come out. She had raised this feline, as she had raised the other one that was one of the pets. This feline had been given to Mekon by Afuan some time back, and Mekon had taught it to attack on command.

"But it was all right when I saw it last," said Jim. "How did this happen to it?"

She drew back a little from him and stared at him, shakily and with surprise.

"Didn't you hear?" she asked. "Afuan left it up to Galyan to fine Mekon for what he'd done. And Galyan decided that the fine

would be . . ." She choked and could not go
on, pointing at the animal.

"It's a strange sort of fine," he said slowly.

"Strange?" She looked up at him puzzledly. "But it's just the sort of fine that
Galyan would exact. He's a demon, Jim.
Where somebody else, operating on the
Princess' orders, might have fined Mekon
one of his favorite servants, or something
else he valued, Galyan chose this poor animal instead—because along with losing it,
of course, Mekon's going to lose a point. Oh,
not a Lifetime Point. Galyan's too clever to
be that hard on someone like Mekon. But
it'll be at least a One-Year Point. And Mekon
has enough points against him already, Lifetime and otherwise, so that he can seriously
worry from time to time about some kind
of an accident that might bring him up to
the level of banishment."

"Banishment?" asked Jim.

"Why, of course. Banishment from the
Throne World—" Ro caught herself suddenly, and wiped her eyes. She stood up
straight and looked down at the body of the
dead animal at her feet. Immediately it
vanished.

"I keep forgetting you don't understand
things," she said, turning to Jim. "There's
so much I'm going to have to teach you. All
the High-born play points. It's one game
that even the Emperor can't overrule; and
too many points means you have to leave
the Throne World forever. But I'll explain it

all to you a little later. Right now I'd better begin teaching you how to move from room to room—"

But Ro's words had woken a new train of thought in Jim's mind.

"Just a second," he said. "Tell me something, Ro. If I wanted to step back into the city right now on an errand before the ship leaves, could I do it?"

"Oh!" she shook her head sadly at him. "I thought you at least knew that. The ship left that outworld world we were on some time ago. We'll be at the Throne World in three ship's-days."

"I see," said Jim grimly.

Her face paled abruptly, and she caught his arms with her hands, as if to keep him from stepping backward from her.

"Don't look like that!" she said. "Whatever it is, you shouldn't look like that!"

Jim forced his face to smooth out. He put away the sudden fury that had exploded inside him. He forced himself to smile down at Ro.

"All right," he said. "I promise you I won't look like that."

Ro still held him by the arms.

"You're so strange," she said, looking up at him. "So strange, in every way. What made you look like that?"

"Something Galyan said to me," he answered. "Something to the effect that I could never go back home again."

"But—you aren't going to want to go back

home!" said Ro, a little wonderingly. "You've never seen the Throne World, so of course you don't know. But no one ever wants to leave it. And the only ones who can stay are the High-born who can keep their point levels down in the Game, and their servants and their possessions. Not even the Governors of the Colony Worlds can do more than visit the Throne World for short periods of time. When their time is up, they have to leave. But the High-born and people like you and me—we can stay."

"I see," he said.

She frowned down at his arms, which she still held. Her fingers were feeling them through the sleeves of his jacket.

"You're as hard-muscled as a Starkien," she said puzzledly. "And you're so tall for someone who's not High-born. Was it natural for you to be this tall back on that wild world you came from?"

Jim laughed a little shortly.

"I was this tall when I was ten years old," he said. The look of slight incomprehension on her face made him add, "That's halfway through my normal growing period."

"And you stopped growing then?" Ro asked.

"I was stopped," he said a little grimly. "Some of our medical practitioners ran a lot of tests on me because I was so big for my age. They couldn't find anything wrong, but they put me on an extract of the pituitary gland to curb my growing. And it worked.

I stopped growing—physically. But I went on growing otherwise."

Jim interrupted himself abruptly. "Never mind that," he said. "You were going to show me how to move around the ship, from room to room."

"That—and other things!" Suddenly she seemed to grow several inches in front of him, and something came into her that was like the cold imperiousness of Princess Afuan. "They can take my animals and give them away or kill them. But they're not going to hurt you. When I get through with you, you'll know more than enough to survive. I may be a throwback, but I'm as High-born as any of them. The Emperor himself can't dismiss me, without cause, from the Throne World; and everything that is High-born's, by right is mine! Come along, and I'll begin to show you what it's like to live among the High-born and be a citizen of the society of the Throne World!"

She took him first to a section of the ship he had not yet visited. It consisted of a large, high-ceilinged, metal-walled room, with one wall covered with the rays of blinking lights of various colors. Tending this wall was one of the short brown men with long hair down his back. He was, Jim discovered, all that the ship possessed in the way of a crew—in fact, he was not even that. In actuality, he was nothing more than a standby engineer, on hand in case of the unlikely chance that some small repair or adjustment needed to be made to the ship's mechanism.

The ship, in fact, ran itself. It not only ran itself, it supplied the motive power for all the transfers of people between rooms, and everything else in the way of visible and invisible equipment aboard. Like some huge robot dog, it responded immediately to the mental whims of the Princess Afuan; and, to a lesser extent, it stood ready to accommodate the whims of everyone else aboard.

"Now," Ro instructed Jim, "simply stand here and relax. Let it make contact with you."

"Make contact with me?" Jim echoed. He assumed that she was talking about something like telepathy, and tried to say so— but found he had no word for it in the Empire language. Ro, however, understood him, and to his considerable surprise, launched into a complete and highly technical explanation of how the ship worked. In brief, it was simply that the ship studied the electrical activity of an individual brain and from this drew up what amounted to an individual electrical code for whatever the person was thinking or doing. Thoughts which were visualized clearly enough, Ro explained, triggered off motor subactivity in the body—in short, the body physically responded at a very low level to the scene it was imagining, as if that scene were real. The ship then matched these responses with the proper scene, and shifted the person to the scene by literally disassembling him at his present position and reassembling him at the location of the imagined scene.

The process by which the ship crossed light-years of empty space was the same method of dissassembly and reassembly, only on a larger scale. That is, the whole ship and its contents were disassembled and reassembled farther along its line of passage. There was a certain limitation to the distance over which one of these shifts could take place, but since each shift took place at computer speeds, the effect was exactly like that of trans-light velocities, without effort.

". . . Actually," wound up Ro, "the ship really never moves at all. It simply changes the coordinates of its position. . . ." And she went off into an explanation too technical for Jim to follow.

Nonetheless, after a little practice at visualization, Jim felt that same sensation—like that of a feather tickling the surface of his mind—that he had felt when Ro had asked him to visualize the warehouse in which his frozen bulls were stored. The first time it happened, he moved from one end of the room he was in to the other. But within minutes after that, he had mastered the knack and was easily shifting from room to room about the ship, although he was restricted to those rooms that he had once seen.

Ro took him back to her quarters, and the social aspects of his education began. The achievements of the few days before they landed on the Throne World surprised both of them. Jim was startled to discover that Ro, like all of the High-born, possessed vast stores of education covering both the scientific and the social aspects of every facet of her ordinary life. It was like her knowledge about the ship. Never in her life would she be called upon to do so much as pay attention to the pattern of winking lights on a ship's control board. But if necessary, she could have built the vessel from scratch, given the necessary tools and materials. Ro, on the other hand, was amazed to discover that she had to tell Jim things only once.

". . . But are you sure you remember that?" she kept interrupting herself to ask Jim. "I never heard of anybody but a High-born who didn't have to work to remember things."

Jim would respond by quoting the last few paragraphs she had said word for word. Reassured, but not really convinced, she would plunge into further detail; and Jim would continue to soak up knowledge about the Throne World, the society of the High-born, and the Empire which Throne World and High-born together ruled.

The picture of it all was beginning to click together for him, as a coherent shape finally emerges after a certain critical number of the pieces of a jigsaw puzzle have been put together. Curiously, the High-born were not direct descendants of those natives of the Throne World who had gone out to colonize the other inhabited worlds of the Empire. They, who were now not merely but in theory rulers of the Empire, had actually come into that position of authority by being weak rather than strong.

It was true that in the beginning the Throne World had tried to keep control of the other worlds it had colonized. But this attempt was soon defeated by the time and space intervening between it and them. Very quickly the newer worlds became autonomous; and by the time, several thousand years later, that the Empire had pushed outward in all directions, until it came to areas where there were no stars with habitable planets within any further reasonable distance, the Throne World had been all but forgotten, except as a birthplace of the human expansion among the stars.

However, even before that expansion had reached its limits, the older colonized worlds had begun to see the advantage of some general organization, some nominal authority and center point which could act as a clearing house for scientific and other developments achieved on other worlds than their own. The Throne World had therefore been revived by common consent and set up as a sort of worldwide combination library and information center. That—though no one

knew it at the time—was the beginning of
the High-born.

To the Throne World, in its new role,
drifted inevitably the better academic and
inventive minds of the Colony Worlds. Here
was the intellectual hub of the human
universe. Here, therefore, it was most profit-
able to live—not only in terms of practical
reward for intellectual labors, but in the
matter of intellectual companionship and
access to new information in one field as
well.

During the next few thousand years this
immigration reached the point that it had
to be restricted by the Throne World itself.
Meanwhile, the Throne World, by virtue of
being the source of supply for most technological advances, had become both rich
and powerful in comparison to the Colony
Worlds. Its intellectual population was already developing into an elite, added to only
sparingly by the best minds of the Colony
Worlds and eagerly served by inhabitants
of the Colony Worlds who were not qualified to join the elite but greatly desired to
live among the mighty.

Eventually, during the last ten thousand
years or so, during which the Empire not
only had remained static but had indeed
shrunk its borders slightly, the Throne
World elite had indeed become High-born—
with special breeding controls which gave
them the physical marks of their aristocracy. The onyx-white skin, the lemon-yellow

eyes, the white hair and eyebrows and eyelashes—all these, Jim learned, were not developed out of any other necessity than to place the badge of superiority upon those who ruled the Empire from the Throne World. Instead of badges or escutcheons to mark their aristocracy, they had given themselves outsize bodies and minds, at the same time ensuring that none who did not belong to their elite could compete with them as individuals. They still gleaned the geniuses and the unusually capable from among what they called the lesser races of man, but that gleaning was highly selective now, and those gleaned did not so much enter the elite themselves as acquire the chance that through inbreeding their great-grandchildren would be one of the tall, white-haired, onyx-skinned masters of the Empire.

". . . You see," Ro said at last to Jim, when they had finally reached the Throne World and were preparing to leave the ship, "there's a chance—even for a Wolfling like you. Oh, they'll try to tear you down, all of the High-born, once they begin to suspect that you want to become one of them. But if you're educated and ready, they won't be able to do it. And with my help, we'll see they won't!"

Her eyes gleamed with triumph. Jim smiled at her and turned the topic of conversation to what he might expect next, once they had left the ship.

She looked suddenly sober.

"I don't know," she said. "Afuan doesn't tell me. Of course, she'll want to show you off to the Emperor as soon as possible."

With this answer in mind, he was consequently at least partly prepared when, an hour or so after the ship had landed on the Throne World, his own room aboard it suddenly vanished around him and he found himself standing in an arena. His luggage was at his feet, and facing him was a complete cuadrilla—banderilleros and picadors, with costumes and horses and all—an exact duplicate of the cuadrilla he had used back on Alpha Centauri III, with the exception that the men in the costumes were all of the breed of short brown men with long, straight hair down their backs.

"These beasts are artificial," said a voice beside him. He turned and saw Afuan standing a few feet from him. "That will include the bull with which you'll be practicing. Both the artificial beast and the men have been set to repeat exactly what you did the time we watched you once before. Simply keep them doing it until they learn how."

The Princess vanished. Apparently she considered that she had said all that needed to be said.

Left alone with his imitation cuadrilla and their mechanical horses, Jim looked around him. The arena was an exact duplicate of the huge arena in which he had fought the two bulls on Alpha Centauri III—

except that it had been cleaned up to an almost ridiculous degree.

The stands of the arena, which on Alpha Centauri III had been of some brown, concretelike material, seemed here to be made of white marble. Everything was white, everywhere—even the sand on the floor of the arena was as white as snow.

Jim bent down, opened one of his luggage cases, and took out the large cape, the small cape, and the sword. He did not bother to take out his costume. He closed the luggage cases and put them behind one of the barreras. Music suddenly began, emanating from some unknown source. It was the right music, and moving with it, Jim lined up before his cuadrilla and began the slow walk across the ring toward a section of seats outlined in red that was plainly the Imperial box.

From Jim's standpoint, it was almost eerie. The longhaired little brown men moved through their motions, not only with professional certainty but also in exact imitation of the men he had left behind on Alpha Centauri III. Even small, useless, personal actions were copied. Evidently all these had been remembered by either Afuan or someone else of the High-born and faithfully fed into whatever programming was controlling the men who were now playing their parts with the bull. Where a man had leaned upon a barrera during an inactive moment, his duplicate here on the Throne World cop-

ied the pose exactly, on the equivalent
barrera, and to an inch of the spot equivalent to where the original had placed his
elbows. But the eeriness of duplication grew
even stronger when Jim went out to work
the bull himself with the large cape. For the
duplication was doubled. There was even
a sort of wry humor to it, thought Jim.
The High-born had produced an imitation
bull, programmed to follow exactly the motions of a live bull they had watched, but
which they did not know had also been
programmed by the biological sciences of
Earth to go through exactly those same
motions.

They carried through the whole business
to the moment of the kill. When Jim's sword
went in, the mechanical creature obediently
collapsed, exactly as the real one had done
back on Alpha Centauri III. Jim looked
around at his pupils, wondering if it was
time to stop; but they seemed quite rested
and evidently were expecting to continue.

It was the second time through the whole
pantomime that Jim began to spare attention from his own work with the imitation
animal to study the actions of the men he
was training. For the first time, he noticed
that although they moved with a great deal
of sureness, there was a certain amount of
clumsiness in their efforts. It was not a clumsiness of the mind as much as the muscles.
These men were doing what they had been
programmed or instructed to do—doing it

promptly and well. But the instinctive responses of their bodies were not yet there.

Jim ran through the complete performance two more times before calling it a day. By that time, although his own responses to the artificial animal had become automatic and without tension, he himself was thoroughly tired. Still, on the succeeding four days he continued to run through the bullfight as it had happened on Alpha Centauri III, until the responses of the small men with the long hair began to be not so much a matter of programming as of experience and natural reflex.

It was somewhere along in this period that he discovered that he could vary the actions of the bull by the same sort of deliberate mental imagery that Ro had taught him to use aboard the ship. Somewhere aboard the Throne World there was a master power source performing the same function for him with regard to the bullring that its counterpart had provided aboard the ship. Therefore, on the sixth day, he introduced his new cuadrilla to a different version of a bullfight.

The truth of the matter was, each of the bulls in cryogenic storage that he had brought with him had been programmed differently—just in case it should be suspected that they had been programmed at all. Jim himself had rehearsed each set of programming. Now he put his new assistants to work in the pattern they would

encounter with the last bull in cryogenic
storage. He used the last bull advisedly,
hoping either that he would never have to
use it in actuality or that his makeshift cuadrilla would have forgotten its specific and
unvarying actions if he did have to use it.

During all these days he had discovered
that he had what appeared to be a suite of
rooms in some endless, one-story structure.
Unlike the rooms aboard ship, the rooms
here on the Throne World had doors and
corridors; moreover, he seemed free to wander about at will, which he did. But though
he explored outward from his rooms through
a number of other parts of the building,
across an open courtyard and through gar-
dens, he encountered no High-born and only
a few other men and women of what were
clearly the lesser races—obviously servants
here on the Throne World.

Ro had not come near him. On the other
hand, Afuan had appeared several times,
inquired briefly as to how the training ses-
sions were coming along, and disappeared
again. She showed neither pleasure nor im-
patience with the time he was taking; but
when the day finally came that he told her
he judged his trainees were ready, her reaction was prompt.

"Excellent!" she said. "You'll put on a
show for the Emperor, then—within the next
day or two."

She disappeared, to return briefly the following morning and announce that the bull-

fight would take place in the arena within a certain span of the Imperial time scale roughly equivalent to about forty minutes.

"I can't get one of my bulls thawed and revived that quickly," Jim said.

"That's already been taken care of," Afuan answered, and disappeared again. Jim began rather hastily to get into his suit of lights. Theoretically, he should have had an assistant help him to dress; but there was no chance for it. He had managed to struggle into about half the costume when the humor of it struck him. He laughed out loud.

"Where are you when I need you, Ro?" he asked the bare white walls of his room humorously. To his utter astonishment, Ro suddenly materialized before him as if she had been a genie summoned from a bottle.

"What do you want me to do?" she demanded.

He stared at her for a second, then laughed again.

"Don't tell me you heard what I said?" he asked her

"Why, yes," she answered, looking a little surprised. "I set up a notice to let me know if you ever called for me. But you never did."

He laughed again. "I'd have called you before this," he said, "if I knew that was all I had to do to get hold of you."

He was treated to the sight of one of her astonishing blushes.

"But I want to help you!" she said. "Only—you didn't seem to be needing any help."

At that he sobered.

"I'm afraid I'm not in the habit of asking for it, usually," he said

"Well, never mind now!" she said energetically. "What do you want me to do?"

"Help me into these clothes," he said. Unexpectedly, she giggled; and he stared at her in puzzlement.

"No, no. It's all right," she said. "It's just that that's the sort of thing a servant, a human of one of the lesser races, is supposed to do for a High-born. Not the other way around."

She picked up his hat.

"Where does this go?" she asked

"It doesn't go—not yet. That's the last item," he told her. Obediently she put it down, and under his instructions began to help him into the rest of the costume.

When he was fully dressed, she looked at him with interest.

"You look strange—but good," she said

"Didn't you see me in the arena at Alpha Centauri III?" he asked.

She shook her head.

"I was busy on the ship—and I really didn't expect it to be too interesting." She stared at him with interest as he took his two capes and sword from the larger luggage case. "What're those for?"

"The pieces of cloth," he said, "are to attract the attention of the bull. The sword"—

he pulled it a little way out of its scabbard to show her its blade—"is to kill him, at the end."

Her hand flew to her mouth. She paled and stepped backward. Her eyes were enormous.

"What's the matter?" he asked.

She tried to say something, but the only sound that came from her throat was more of a little cry than an understandable word. He frowned sharply

"What is it?" he demanded. "What's wrong?"

"You didn't tell me . . ." The words came out of her, finally, in a sort of wail. "You didn't tell me you were going to *kill* him!"

She choked, whirled about, and disappeared. He stood staring at the space where she had been. Behind him a woman's voice spoke unexpectedly.

"Yes," it said. It was the voice of Princess Afuan, and he himself turned sharply, to find her standing there looking at him. "It seems that even a Wolfling like you can make mistakes. I'd have thought you'd have learned by this time that Ro has a soft spot in her for all animals."

He looked at her coldly.

"You're right," he said flatly; "I should've remembered that."

"Unless," she said, then paused, watching him with her lemon-yellow eyes, "that is, you had some reason for deliberately wanting to upset her. You've made quite a

marked impression for a Wolfling, in such a
short time. You not only made a friend of
little Ro, but you made an enemy of Mekon,
and interested not only Slothiel, but Galyan
himself."

She considered him for a second with a
close gaze that seemed to have something
hidden in it

"Do you see me?"

"Of course," he said. And then he stiffened internally, although he was careful to
keep his face and body noncommittal.

For, before his eyes Afuan suddenly
changed. It was a strange changing, because
no single thing about her that he could see
altered in any way. Even the expression on
her face was the same. But suddenly she
was entirely different.

Suddenly, tall, onyx-skinned, yellow-eyed,
white-haired as she was, she became attractive. No—not merely attractive—voluptuous
to an almost overwhelming degree. It was
more than merely a sensual attraction she
projected. Her demand upon his capability
of desire was almost hypnotic.

Only the long, solitary years of internal
isolation and growth allowed him to resist
the fascination Afuan was now exerting upon
him. Only the fact that he realized the lust
she was trying to awaken in him meant an
abandonment of all that he had searched
for and won by lonely journeys of the mind
and soul, where the mind and soul of man
had never searched before—only this allowed

him to stand still, relaxed and calm, unresponsive.

Abruptly, again without any phsysical sign of change, Afuan was back as she had always been. Cold and remote in appearance, striking, but not necessarily attractive by the human standards of Earth.

"Amazing," she said a little softly, gazing at him through eyes which—though they were not slitted—gave the impression of being slitted. "Totally amazing, particularly for a Wolfling. But I think I understand you now, wild man. Something in you, at some time, has made you ambitious with an ambition larger than the universe."

After a second Jim performed the mental exercise that transferred him to the arena.

When he appeared there, the stands were already full of the white-clothed High-born. Not only that, but within the red-bordered area that was plainly the Imperial box was a party of six men and four women. The music had already begun, and Jim formed up with his cuadrilla for the walk across the white sand toward the Imperial box. As he got close, he saw that Afuan was one of the people in the box, seated to the left of someone who seemed to be Galyan, who was occupying the center seat, with an unusually broad-bodied, older-looking High-born man to his right, who had slightly yellowed eyebrows.

When Jim got close to the box, however, he saw that the man who resembled Galyan was not Galyan. Still, the resemblance was striking, and Jim suddenly remembered Galyan's comment about the Emperor being his first cousin. This, plainly, was the Emperor.

If anything, he was taller than Galyan himself. He lounged in his seat more casually than the other High-born seated around him, and there was something—for a High-born—unusually frank and open and intelligent about his gaze. He smiled down at Jim as he gave permission for the bullfight to commence. Afuan's eyes looked coldly down at Jim meanwhile

Jim had eliminated the procedure of dedicating the bull to someone in the audience, and he did not revive the practice now. He returned with his cuadrilla across the ring and went directly into the bullfight. His men did well with the different behavior of the bull, which Afuan or someone else among the High-born had apparently chosen to revive at random from among the six in cryogenic storage. Luckily, each bull was a little different, and Jim recognized the differences, so that he was able to adjust himself to the bull's pattern of behavior the minute he saw it come charging into the ring.

Still, he had his hands full with it, as he had had his hands full in the arena on Alpha Centauri III. Moreover, what little space for thought he had was taken up with Afuan's comment about his ambition. Clearly the Princess possessed a sense of perception that was very nearly deadly.

The bullfight continued, and drew eventually to its closing moments. This bull, unlike the one on Alpha Centauri III, remained strong right up to the predicted point in its programming. Jim finally went in over the horns with his sword for the kill, almost directly in front of the Imperial box. Then, withdrawing his sword, he turned and took a few steps to confront the Emperor—as much from his own sense of interest in how the Emperor would respond to the spectacle as for the reason that on the ship Ro had told him that approaching the Emperor afterward would be expected of him. He walked up to the barrier itself and looked upward at a slant into the face of the Emperor, less than a dozen feet away. The Emperor smiled down. His eyes seemed to shine with an unusual brightness—although suddenly Jim noticed there was something almost unfocused about them

The Emperor's smile broadened. A small trickle of saliva ran down from one corner of his mouth. He opened his lips and spoke to Jim.

"Waw," he said, smiling all the while and staring directly through Jim. "Waw. . . ."

Chapter 5

Jim stood still. There was nothing to give him a clue as to how he should react. The rest of the High-born in the Imperial box—in fact, all the High-born within view—seemed deliberately to be paying no attention at all to whatever fit or stroke had suddenly taken the Emperor. Plainly, Jim judged that he would be expected to ignore it also. Afuan and all the others in the royal box merely sat as if the Emperor was in fact engaged in a private conversation with Jim. In fact, so persuasive and so massive was the reaction, which was *no* reaction, that it had something of the same hypnotic compulsion that Afuan had used earlier, except that in this case it seemed determined to convince not only Jim but also themselves that what was happening to the Emperor was not happening.

Then, suddenly, it was all over.

The saliva vanished from the Emperor's jaw as if an invisible hand had wiped it away. His smile firmed, his eyes focused.

". . . Moreover, we are exceedingly interested to know more about you," the Emperor was suddenly saying, as if continuing a conversation that had been going on for some time. "You are the first Wolfling we have seen in many years here at our court. After you have rested, you must come to see us, and we'll have a talk."

The Emperor's smile was open, frank, and charming. His voice was friendly, his eyes intelligent.

"Thank you, Oran," replied Jim. He had been instructed by Ro that the Emperor was always referred to as "the Emperor" in every way except direct address; when one was speaking to him directly, one always called him simply by his first name—Oran.

"You're entirely welcome," said the Emperor, smiling cheerfully. He vanished, and a second later all the seats in the stands were empty of High-born.

Jim visualized his own quarters and was instantly back in them. Thoughtfully, he began to remove his costume. He was struggling out of the tight jacket when he suddenly felt himself assisted from behind, and looking around, saw Ro helping him.

"Thank you," he said, and smiled over his shoulder at her as the jacket came off. She went on helping him, her eyes fixed on the floor; but a dark flush stained her downcast features.

"I still think it's terrible!" she muttered to the floor. "But I didn't realize—" Suddenly she lifted her face to him, paling again.

"I really didn't realize, Jim. That animal was trying to kill *you*."

"Yes," said Jim, feeling once more the secret, internal touch of shame that came to him whenever he remembered how his bullfighting was rigged, rather than honest. "That's the way it is."

"Anyway," said Ro in very nearly a grim tone of voice, "if we're lucky, you won't ever have to do it again. It's a stroke of luck, to start off with, the Emperor being interested in you. And—guess what?"

She stopped assisting him, and he stood there, half-undressed, staring quizzically down at her.

"What?" he asked.

"I've found a sponsor for you!" she burst out excitedly. "Slothiel! He liked you when you didn't flinch—that first time he saw you. And he's willing to have you numbered among his acquaintances. Do you know what that means?"

She stopped and waited for his answer. He shook his head. What she was talking about now was something she had not gone into aboard the ship.

"It means you're not really in the servant class from now on!" she burst out. "I'd hoped to get someone to sponsor you—but not this soon. And I didn't want to raise your hopes by mentioning it. But Slothiel actually came to me!"

"He did?" Jim frowned internally, although he was careful to keep his physical brow smooth for Ro's benefit. He wondered if Slothiel had anything to do with Afuan's visit to him earlier—or what Galyan had said to him aboard the ship. He found himself on the verge of asking Ro this, and then he changed his mind. Afuan's visit, and the reaction she had tried to provoke in him, he found, was not something he wanted to tell Ro about—at least, not just yet.

He came out of his thoughts abruptly, to realize that Ro was still busily undressing him, with no apparent self-consciousness about the matter. He had no great self-consciousness about it himself. But Ro's attitude struck him just then as being a little too zealously proprietary, like that of an owner lovingly grooming a pet horse or dog for show purposes. Besides, Jim had needed assistance, not complete care and handling.

"That's fine," he said, moving out of her grasp. "I can handle the rest of it myself."

He picked up his Black Watch kilt from the hassock on which he had dropped it when he had hastily started to dress for the bullring. He put it on, together with a short-sleeved green shirt. Ro watched him with fond pride.

"Tell me more about this sponsorship business," said Jim; "sponsorship for what?"

"Why," said Ro, opening her eyes wide, "for adoption by the Throne World, of course! Don't you remember? I told you that still, occasionally, a few rare people of unusual abilities or talents are allowed to move from one of the Colony Worlds to the Throne World and join the High-born. Though, of course, they aren't really High-born themselves; the best they can hope for is that their great-grandchildren will become true High-born. Well, that whole process is called adoption by the Throne World. And adoption proceedings start by someone among the High-born being willing to act as sponsor to whomever wants to be adopted."

"You're thinking of getting me adopted as a High-born?" asked Jim, smiling a little.

"Of course not!" Ro literally hugged herself with glee. "But, once you've been sponsored, the adoption proceedings have been started. And you're protected by the Emperor's authority as a provisional High-born, until he gets around to either accepting you or refusing you. And the thing is, nobody ever gets refused, once he's been sponsored, unless he's done something so bad that there's no alternative but to get him off the Throne World. Once Slothiel sponsors you, none of the High-born can do anything to you the way they can to a servant. I mean, your life's protected. None of the High-born—not even Afuan or Galyan—can simply act against you. They have to complain about you to the Emperor."

"I see," said Jim thoughtfully. "Should I mention that Slothiel is going to do this when I talk to the Emperor?"

"Talk to the Emperor?" Ro stared at him and then burst out laughing. But she stopped quickly and put an apologetic hand on his arm. "I'm sorry. I shouldn't have laughed. But the chances are you'll spend your whole life here and never talk to the Emperor."

"The chances are wrong, then," said Jim, "because after the bullfight the Emperor asked me to come and see him as soon as I'd had a chance to rest a bit."

Ro stared at him. Then slowly she shook her head.

"You don't understand, Jim," she said sympathetically. "He just said that. Nobody *goes* to see the Emperor. The only time they see him is when he has them brought to him. If you're going to see the Emperor, you'll suddenly find yourself brought into his presence. Until then, you just have to wait." Jim frowned.

"I'm sorry, Jim," she said. "You didn't know it, but the Emperor often says things like that. But then, something else comes up and he forgets all about it. Or else he just says it without meaning it, just because it's something to say. Like paying a compliment."

Jim smiled slowly, and Ro's face paled again.

"Don't look like that!" she said, catching hold of his arm again. "No one should look savage like that."

"Don't worry," said Jim. He erased the grin. "But I'm afraid you're wrong. I'm going to see the Emperor. Where would he be?"

"Why, in Vhotan's office, this time of day—" She broke off suddenly, staring at him. "Jim, you mean it! Don't you understand? You can't go there—"

"Just show me the way," said Jim.

"I won't!" she said. "He'd order his Starkiens to kill you! Maybe they'd even kill you without waiting to be ordered."

"Oh? And why would the Starkiens want to kill our wild man?" broke in Slothiel's voice unexpectedly. They turned to discover that the tall High-born had just materialized in the room with them. Ro wheeled upon him as if he were the cause of her argument with Jim.

"After the bullfight the Emperor told Jim to rest awhile, then come and see him!" said Ro. "Now Jim wants me to tell him how to get to the Emperor! I told him I won't do it!"

Slothiel broke out laughing.

"*Go* to the Emperor!" he echoed. "Well, why don't you tell him? If you won't, I will."

"True," drawled Slothiel, "and I will—because I admire the man and because I'll enjoy the look on Galyan's face when he hears about it. But if—what did you say his name is—Jim is bound and determined to get himself killed before the sponsorship can be arranged, who am I to interfere with his fate?"

He looked at Jim over the head of Ro,

who had pushed herself between them.

"You really want to go?" Slothiel said.

Jim smiled again grimly.

"I'm a Wolfling," he said. "I don't know any better."

"Right," said Slothiel, ignoring Ro's frantic attempts to silence him by her voice and her hand over his mouth. "Hang on. I'll send you there. For all the Emperor and Vhotan will know, you found the way yourself."

Immediately, Jim was in a different room. It was a very large circular room with some sort of transparent ceiling showing a cloud-flecked sky above—or was the sky with its clouds merely an illusion overhead? Jim had no time to decide which, because his attention was all taken up by the reaction of the half-dozen people already in the room, who had just caught sight of him.

Of the half-dozen men in the room, one was the Emperor. He had checked himself in mid-sentence on seeing Jim appear; and he stood half-turned from the older, powerfully bodied High-born who had sat at his right during the bullfight. Standing back a little way from these two, with his back to Jim, and just now turning to see what had interrupted the Emperor, was a male High-born whom Jim did not recognize. The other three men in the room were heavily muscled, gray-skinned, bald-headed individuals like

the one Galyan had referred to as his bodyguard. These wore leather loin straps, with
a black rod thrust through loops in the belt
around their waist, and about the rest of
their body and limbs were metallic-looking
bands, which, however, seemed to fit and
cling to position on them more like bands
of thick elastic cloth than metal. At the
sight of Jim, they had immediately drawn
their rods and were aiming them at him
when a sharp, single word from the Emperor stopped them.

"No!" said the Emperor. "It's—" He
seemed to peer at Jim without recognition
for a second; then a broad smile spread
across his face. "Why, it's the Wolfling!"

"Exactly!" snapped the older High-born.
"And what's he doing here? Nephew, you'd
better—"

"Why," interupted the Emperor, striding
toward Jim, still smiling broadly at him, "I
invited him here. Don't you remember,
Vhotan? I issued the invitation after the
bullfight."

Already the Emperor's tall body was between Jim and the three thick-bodied, armed
bodyguards. He stopped one of his own long
paces away from Jim and stood smiling
down at him.

"Naturally," the Emperor said, "you came
as soon as you could, didn't you, Wolfling?
So as not to offend us by keeping us waiting?"

"Yes, Oran," answered Jim.

But now the older man, called Vhotan, who was apparently the Emperor's uncle, had come up to stand beside his nephew. His lemon-yellow eyes under their yellowish tufts of eyebrows glared down at Jim.

"Nephew," he said, "you can't possibly let this wild man get away with something like this. Break protocol once, and you set a precedent for a thousand repetitions of the same thing!"

"Now, now, Vhotan," said the Emperor, turning his smile appeasingly on the older High-born. "How many Wolflings have we on our Throne World who don't yet know the palace rules? No, I invited him here. If I remember, I even said I might find him interesting to talk to; and now, I believe I might."

He stepped aside, and folded himself up, sitting down on one of the large hassocklike pillows that played the role of furniture for the High-born.

"Sit down, Wolfling," he said. "You too, Uncle—and you, Lorava—" He glanced aside at the third High-born, a slim, younger male who had just come up. "Let's all sit down here together and have a chat with the Wolfling. Where do you come from, Wolfling? Out toward galaxy's-edge of our Empire, isn't it?"

"Yes, Oran," Jim answered. He had already seated himself; and reluctantly Vhotan was lowering himself to a hassock beside the Emperor. The young High-born called Lorava took two hasty strides up to them and also sat down on a nearby pillow.

"A lost colony. A lost world," mused the Emperor, almost to himself, "filled with wild men—and no doubt wilder beasts?"

He looked at Jim for an answer.

"Yes," said Jim, "we still have a good number of wild beasts—although that number's been reduced, in the last few hundred years particularly. Man has a tendency to crowd out the wild animals."

"Man has a tendency to crowd out even man, sometimes," said the Emperor. For a moment a little shadow seemed to pass behind his eyes, as if he remembered some private sadness of his own. Jim watched him with careful interest. It was hard to believe that this man before him was the same one he had seen drooling and making incoherent sounds in the arena.

"But the men there—and the women. Are they all like you?" the Emperor said, returning the focus of his eyes to Jim.

"Each one of us is different, Oran," said Jim.

The Emperor laughed.

"Of course!" he said. "And no doubt, being healthy wild men, you prize the difference, instead of trying to fit yourselves all into one common mold. Like we superior beings, we High-born of the Throne World!" His humor calmed slightly. "How did we happen to find your world, after having lost it so many centuries—or thousands of years—ago?"

"The Empire didn't find us," said Jim. "We found an outlying world of the Empire."

There was a second's silence in the room, broken by a sudden half-snort, half-bray of laughter from the youngster Lorava.

"He's lying!" Lorava sputtered. "They found us? If they could find us, how did they ever get lost in the first place?"

"Quiet!" snapped Vhotan at Lorava. He turned back to Jim. His face and the face of the Emperor were serious. "Are you telling us that your people, after forgetting about the Empire, and the falling back into complete savagery, turned around and developed civilization all over again—including a means of space travel?"

"Yes," said Jim economically.

Vhotan stared hard into Jim's eyes for a long second, and then turned to the Emperor.

"It might be worth checking, Nephew," he said.

"Worth checking. Yes . . ." murmured the Emperor. But his thoughts seemed to have wandered. He was no longer gazing at Jim, but off across the room at nothing in particular; and a look of gentle melancholy had taken possession of his face. Vhotan glanced at him and then got to his feet. The older High-born stepped over to Jim, tapped him on the shoulder with a long forefinger, and beckoned for him to rise.

Jim got to his feet. Behind the still-seated, still abstractedly gazing Emperor, Lorava also rose to his feet. Vhotan led them both quietly to a far end of the room, then turned to Lorava.

"I'll call you back later, Lorava," he said brusquely.

Lorava nodded and disappeared. Vhotan turned back to Jim.

"We've had an application from Slothiel to sponsor you for adoption," Vhotan said quickly. "Also, you were brought here by the Princess Afuan; and I understand you had some contact with Galyan. Are all of those things correct?"

"They are," said Jim.

"I see. . . ." Vhotan stood for a second, his eyes hooded thoughtfully. Then his gaze sharpened once more upon Jim. "Did any of those three suggest that you come here just now?"

"No," answered Jim. He smiled slightly at the tall, wide-shouldered old man towering massively over him. "Coming here was my own idea—in response to the Emperor's invitation. I only mentioned it to two other people. Slothiel and Ro."

"Ro?" Vhotan frowned. "Oh, that little girl, the throw-back in Afuan's household. You're sure *she* didn't suggest your coming here?"

"Perfectly sure. She tried to stop me," said Jim. "And as for Slothiel—when I told him I was coming, he laughed."

"Laughed?" Vhotan echoed the word, then grunted. "Look at my eyes, Wolfling!"

Jim fastened his own gaze on the two lemon-yellow eyes under the slightly yellowish tufts of eyebrows. As he gazed, the eyes seemed to increase in brilliance and swim before him in the old man's face, until they threatened to merge.

"How many eyes do I have?" he heard Vhotan's voice rumbling.

Two eyes swam together, like two yellowish-green suns, burning before him. They tried to become one. Jim felt a pressure upon him like that of the hypnotic influence Afuan had tried to bring to bear on him before the bullfight. He stiffened internally, and the eyes separated.

"Two," he said.

"You're wrong, Wolfling," said Vhotan. "I have one eye. One eye only!"

"No," said Jim. The two eyes remained separate. "I see two."

Vhotan grunted again. Abruptly his gaze ceased burning down upon Jim, and the hypnotic pressure relaxed.

"Well, I see I'm not going to find out that way," said Vhotan, almost to himself. His gaze sharpened upon Jim again, but in an ordinary rather than a hypnotic fashion. "But I suppose you understand that I can easily find out if you've been telling the truth or not."

"I assumed you could," said Jim.

"Yes. . . ." Vhotan became thoughtful

again. "There's a good deal more here than surface indication implies. . . . Let's see, the Emperor can act on Slothiel's application for sponsorship, of course. But I think you'll need more than that. Let's see. . . ."

Vhotan turned his head abruptly to the right and spoke to empty air.

"Lorava!"

The thin young High-born appeared.

"The Emperor is appointing this Wolfling to an Award Commission as unit officer in the Starkiens. See to the details and his assignment to a section of the palace guard . . . . And send Melness to me."

Lorava disappeared again. About three seconds later another, smaller man materialized where he had stood.

He was a slim, wiry man in typical white tunic and kilt with close-cropped reddish hair and a skin that would almost have matched the color of Jim's own if there had not been a sort of sallow, yellowish tinge to it. His face was small and sharp-featured, and the pupils of his eyes were literally black. He was clearly not one of the High-born but there was an air of assurance and authority about him which transcended that even of the armed bodyguard called Starkiens.

"Melness," said Vhotan, "this man is a Wolfling—the one that just put on the spectacle in the arena a few hours ago."

Melness nodded. His black eyes flickered

from Vhotan to Jim, and back to the tall old High-born once more.

"The Emperor is appointing him to an Award Commission in the Starkiens of the palace guard. I've told Lorava to take care of the assignment but I'd like you to see to it that his duties are made as nominal as possible."

"Yes, Vhotan," answered Melness. His voice was a hardedged, masculine tenor. "I'll take care of it—and him."

He vanished, in his turn. Vhotan looked once more at Jim

"Melness is majordomo of the palace," Vhotan said. "In fact, he's in charge, at least in theory, of all those not High-born on the Throne World. If you have any difficulties, see him. Now, you can return to your own quarters. And don't come here again unless you're sent for!"

Jim visualized the room where he had left Ro and Slothiel. He felt the slight feather touch on his mind, and at once he was back there.

Both of them, he saw, were still there. Ro rushed at him the minute she saw him and threw her arms around him. Slothiel laughed.

"So you came back," said the languid High-born. "I had a hunch you would. In fact, I offered to bet on the point with Ro. here—but she's not the betting kind. What happened to you?"

"I've been given an Award Commission in

the Starkiens," said Jim calmly. His eyes met Slothiel's. "And Vhotan tells me that the Emperor will act promptly upon your offer to sponsor me."

Ro let go of him and stepped backward, staring up at him in astonishment. Slothiel condescended to raise his eyebrows in surprise.

"Jim!" said Ro in a wondering tone. "What— what *did* happen?"

Briefly Jim told them. When he was done, Slothiel whistled admiringly and cheerfully.

"Excuse me," he said. "This looks like a good chance to clean up on a few small bets before the rest of the Throne World hears about your promotions."

He disappeared. Ro, however, had not moved. Looking down at her, Jim saw that her face was tightened by lines of worry.

"Jim," she said hesitantly, "Vhotan did ask exactly that about me, did he? . . . About whether I might've suggested that you go to the Emperor that way? And he asked that after he remembered that I was in Afuan's household?"

"That's right," said Jim. He smiled a little bleakly. "Interesting, isn't it?"

Ro shivered suddenly

"No, it isn't!" she said tensely but in a low voice. "It's frightening! I knew I could teach you things and help you survive here in the ordinary way. But if things are going on in which others of the High-born want to use you. . . ." Her voice trailed off. Her eyes were dark with unhappiness.

Jim considered her in silence for a moment. Then he spoke.

"Ro," he said, slowly, "tell me. Is the Emperor ill?"

She looked up at him in astonishment.

"Ill? . . . You mean, sick?" she said. Then, suddenly, she laughed. "Jim, none of the High-born are ever sick—least of all the Emperor."

"There's something wrong with him," said Jim. "And it can't be much of a secret if it happens the way it happened in the arena after the bullfight. Did you see how he changed when he started to speak to me after the bull was dead?"

"Changed?" She literally stared at him. "Changed? In what way?"

Jim told her.

". . . You didn't see how he looked, or hear the sounds he made?" asked Jim. "Of course not—come to think of it, you probably weren't sitting that close."

"But, Jim!" She put her hand on his arm in that familiar, persuasive gesture of hers. "Every seat in the arena there has its own focusing equipment. Why, when you were fighting with that animal"—she shuddered briefly, in passing, then hurried on—"I could see you from as closely as I wanted, as if I were standing as close to you as I am now. When you turned toward the Imperial box, I was still focused right in on you. I saw the

Emperor speak to you, and if he'd done
anything out of the ordinary, I'd have noticed it too!"

He stared at her.

"You didn't see what I saw?" he said after a second.

She continued to meet his eyes in a pattern of honesty; but with a sudden sensitiv-
ity inside himself, he seemed to feel that,
within, she was somehow refusing to meet
his eye—without being really aware of this
herself.

"No," she said. "I saw him speak to you
and heard him invite you to visit him after
you'd had a chance to rest. Nothing more
than that."

She continued to stand, gazing up into
his eyes in that pattern of exterior honesty,
with the inner aversion of her gaze unknown
to her but evident to him. The seconds
stretched out, and he suddenly realized that
she was fixed. She was incapable of breaking the near-trance of this moment. He
would have to be the one to interrupt it.

He turned his head away from her and
was just in time to see the gray-skinned,
bald-headed figure of a Starkien appear in
the room about five feet away from them.

Jim stiffened, staring at him.

"Who are you?" Jim demanded.

"My name is Adok I," responded the new-
comer. "But I am you."

Chapter 6

Jim frowned sharply at the man, who, however, showed no reaction to his frown at all.

"You're me?" Jim echoed. "I don't understand."

"Why, Jim!" broke in Ro. "He's your substitute, of course. You can't actually be a Starkien yourself. Any more than a—" She fumbled for a parallel and gave it up. "Well, look at him. And look at yourself!" she finished.

"The High-born is quite right," said Adok I. He had a deep, flat, emotionless voice. "Award Commissions are usually given to those who are not Starkien by birth and training. In such cases a substitute is always provided."

"A substitute is, is he?" said Jim. "In that case, what do they call you officially, in the records?"

"Officially, as I said, I'm you," answered Adok I.

"Officially, my name is James Keil. I am a Wolfling from a world that calls itself"

86

—the Starkien's tongue stumbled a little with the pronunciation of the unknown word—"Earth."

"I thought you told me that you were Adok I," Jim said. The extreme seriousness of the Starkien was tempting him to smile, but an instinct kept the smile hidden within him and off his face

"Unofficially, to you, Jim," said the other man, "I am Adok I. Your intimates, like the High-born lady here, may call me either Adok I or Jim Keil—it makes no difference."

"I'll call you Adok I," said Ro. "And you can call me Ro."

"I'll do that, Ro," said Adok I in a tone of voice as if he were repeating an order he had just been given, and affirming his willingness and ability to execute it.

Jim shook his head, amused and intrigued by the combination of characteristics the Starkien was exhibiting. The man seemed humorless to the point of woodenness, obedient to the point of servility, and in conjunction with these things, evidently considered it the best possible manners to address Jim by the familiar short form of Jim's first name. Moreover, beyond this, Adok I seemed to assume a strange mixture of superiority and inferiority toward Jim at the same time. Clearly the Starkien did not for a moment appear to consider that Jim had the capabilities to perform the tasks that Adok I was himself fitted to perform. On the other hand, plainly he considered himself completely a creature of Jim's will—at Jim's beck and call. However, thought Jim abruptly, investigation of Adok's character could come later. There was a more immediate question.

"Well," Jim said, "now that I've got you, what am I supposed to do with you?"

"We should begin with my doing things with you, Jim," said Adok I. He looked over at Ro. "If Ro will excuse us, I should immediately begin instructing you in the necessities and duties of being a unit officer—over and above those in which I can substitute for you."

"I've got to get back to my pets anyway," said Ro. "I'll come and find you later, Jim."

She touched him lightly on the arm and disappeared.

"All right, Adok," said Jim, turning back to the Starkien, "what do we do first?"

"We should begin with a visit to the quarters of your unit," Adok said. "If you will allow me to show you the way, Jim—"

"Go ahead," said Jim, and immediately found himself with Adok in what seemed to be an enormous, windowless, high-ceilinged room. In spite of all that space, however, something within Jim felt the sensation of closeness, an oppression as of confinement.

"Where are we?" he asked Adok, for the polished floor stretching away from them was empty in all directions for large distances, except for a few distant moving figures almost lost in the dimness and distance.

"We're at the parade ground." Adok's head came around to gaze at Jim with the first faint sign of emotion the Starkien had yet shown. After a second Jim realized Adok was registering surprise. "We are also below ground." Adok gave their depth in Empire terms, which translated to something like half a mile down from the surface of the planet. "Does it disturb you? It disturbs the High-born, but only a few of the servants are disturbed by it."

"No, I'm not disturbed," Jim said. "I felt something, though."

"If you are disturbed, you should admit it to me," said Adok. "If you are ever afraid or disturbed, you should tell me, even if you tell no one else. No one else but I need to know. But it is necessary for me to know when you are emotionally weakened, so that I can take measures to protect you from such weakness and hide the fact from others."

Jim chuckled, and the sound echoed eerily away into the distances around them. It was an odd moment and place for humor, but Jim was finding Adok I strangely likeable.

"Don't worry," he told the Starkien. "I don't usually feel emotionally weakened. But if I ever do, I promise to let you know."

"Good," said Adok seriously. "Now I brought you first to this point on the parade ground because one of the things I cannot do for you is stand certain parades with the unit. At some parades we both must be present. Now that you have been brought to this spot, you can instantly return to it on your own in case something may have made you a little late in showing up for the parade. Now, let's go to the armory, and we'll draw your weapons and accouterments while you memorize that destination also."

The next room they appeared in was more brightly lit and a very great deal smaller than the parade ground. It was a long narrow room, both long walls of which seemed to be divided into compartments holding the leather straps and the bands of silver stuff such as those which encircle the legs, arms, and body of Adok, as well as those of the Starkiens in the room with the Emperor and Vhotan. Adok led Jim directly to several of the compartments and collected an assortment of the straps and silver bands. He did not, however, suggest that Jim put them on at this time. Instead, Adok himself carried them, while he transported Jim in quick succession to the barracks, or living quarters, of the Starkiens in Jim's unit— these were suites of rooms not unlike those that Jim himself had been given, except that they were smaller and in this below-ground location; a gymnasium; a dining hall; a sort of underground park, with grass and trees flourishing under an artificial sun; and finally to a sort of amusement and shopping center, where many Starkiens mingled with many times more their own number of other servants of the lesser races.

Finally Adok concluded the quick shift about these various locations by bringing Jim to a large room fitted out somewhat like the room in which Jim had encountered the Emperor and Vhotan. Not only was it large and well furnished, but Jim instantly felt a lightening of the sensation within him that had warned him before that he was below ground. Apparently this room, whatever it was, was above ground.

"Who—" he began to Adok, and then found his question answered before he could enunciate it. The olive-skinned man called Melness materialized in front of them and looked, not at Jim, but at Adok.

"I have taken him around the places concerned with his unit," Adok said to the Master Servant of the Throne World, "and brought him here finally to you, as you asked, Melness."

"Good," said Melness in his sharp tenor. His black eyes flicked to Jim's face. "The sponsorship for your adoption has been accepted by the Emperor."

"Thanks for telling me," said Jim.

"I'm not telling you for your benefit," said Melness, "but because it's necessary for me to make your situation clear to you. As a candidate for adoption, you are in theory a probationary High-born, who is superior to me, as to all servants. On the other hand, as an officer of the Starkiens below the rank of a Ten-unit Commander, as well as because you were born among one of the lesser races of man, you are under my orders."

Jim nodded.

"I see," he said.

"I hope you do!" said Melness sharply. "We have a contradiction; and the way such contradictions are resolved is to accord you with two official personalities. That is, any activity, occupation, or duty which you deal with in your capacity as a candidate for adoption invokes your personality as a probationary High-born, and my personal superior. On the other hand, any activity which deals with your duties as an officer of the Starkiens invokes your servant personality; and you are my inferior in everything connected with that. In any activities that deal with neither personality officially, you can choose which position you want to occupy—High-born or servant. I don't imagine you'll want to choose the servant often."

"I don't suppose so," said Jim, watching the smaller man calmly. The black eyes flickered upon him like dark flashes of lightning.

"Because of the conflict of personalities," said Melness, "I have no physical authority over you. But if necessary, I can suspend you from duty with your Starkien unit and enter a formal complaint to the Emperor about you. Don't let yourself be misled by any foolish notion that the Emperor will not act upon any complaint I make to him."

"I won't," said Jim softly. Melness looked at him for a moment more, then disappeared.

"Now, Jim," Adok said at his elbow, "if you like, we can return to your quarters; and I will show you the use of your weapons and accouterments."

"Fine," said Jim.

They transported themselves back to Jim's quarters. There Adok fitted Jim out with the straps and belts he had brought from the armory.

"There are two classes of weaponry," said Adok, once Jim was outfitted. "This"—he tapped the small black rod he had inserted in the loops of the belt attached to Jim's loin strap—"is independently powered and is all that is normally used for duty upon the Throne World."

He paused and then reached out softly to touch a silver band encircling the biceps of Jim's upper left arm.

"These, however," said Adok, "are part of the weaponry of the second class. They are completely useless at the moment, because they must be energized by a broadcast power source. Each of them is both a weapon and an enabler at the same time."

"Enabler?" Jim asked.

"Yes," said Adok. "They increase your reflex time, by causing you to react physically at a certain set speed—which in the case of anyone not High-born is considerably above his natural speed of reflex. Later on, we'll be working out with the enabler function of the second-class weaponry. And eventually, perhaps you can get permission to go to the testing area, which is at a good distance below the surface of the Throne World, and gain some actual experience with the weapons themselves."

"I see," said Jim, examining the silver bands. "I take it, then, that they're fairly powerful?"

"A trained Starkien," said Adok, "under full control of effective second-class weaponry, should be the equivalent of two to six units of fully armed men from the Colony Worlds."

"The Colony Worlds don't have Starkiens of their own, then?" asked Jim.

For a second time Adok managed to register a mildly visible emotion. This time the emotion seemed to be shock.

"The Starkiens serve the Emperor—and only the Emperor!" he said.

"Oh?" said Jim. "On the ship that brought me to the Throne World, I had a talk with a High-born named Galyan. And Galyan had a Starkien—or somebody who looked exactly like a Starkien—bodyguarding him."

"There's nothing strange in that, Jim," said Adok. "The Emperor lends his Starkiens to the other High-born when the other Highborn need them. But they are only lent. They still remain servants of the Emperor, and in the final essential their commands come only from the Emperor."

Jim nodded. Adok's words rang an echo off the remembered words of Melness a short time before. Jim's thoughts ran on ahead with the connection.

"The underground area on the Throne World is occupied only by the servants, is that right, Adok?" he asked.

"As long as I'm going to be going down there as a matter of duty from now on," said Jim, "I think I'd like to see some more of it. How large an area is it?"

"There are as many rooms below grounds," said Adok, "as there are above. In fact, there may be more, because I don't know them all."

"Who does?" asked Jim.

Adok looked for a second as though he would have shrugged. But the gesture was evidently too marked a one for him to make.

"I don't know, Jim," he said. "Perhaps . . . Melness."

"Yes," said Jim thoughtfully. "Of course, if anyone would know, it would be Melness.

During the next few weeks Jim found himself involved in several parades down on the parade grounds. He discovered that his duties on these occasions were nothing more than to get dressed and to stand before his unit, which consisted of seventy-eight Starkiens, a noncommissioned Starkien officer, Adok, and himself

But the first parade he witnessed, it came as a shock to him to see that vast space underground completely filled with rank upon rank of the impassive, bald-headed, short, and massive-boned men who were the Starkiens. Jim had assumed that the Throne World was a full-sized planetary body, that there would be a large number of servants and all types, and that the Starkiens should be a fair proportion of these. But he had not realized, until he saw it with his own eyes, how many Starkiens there were. A little calculation afterward based upon what Adok could tell him of the floor space of the parade ground area led him to estimate that he must have seen at least twenty thousand men under arms in that space.

If it was indeed true, what Adok said, that each Starkien was the equivalent of four to five times a unit of eighty soldiers from the Colony Worlds, then what he had seen gathered there had been the equivalent of between half and three-quarters of a million men. —And Adok had told him that this parade ground was only one of fifty spaced about the Throne World, underground.

Perhaps it was not so surprising that the High-born of the Throne World considered themselves above any threat that could be posed by any Colony World or combination of Colony Worlds.

Outside the parades, Jim found that his only duties during the first few weeks consisted of a session in the gymnasium every other day with Adok, wearing the second-class weaponry.

The silver bands that represented the second-class weaponry were still not energized as weapons, but within the confines of the gymnasium they became active in their capacity as enablers. The exercises that Jim was put through by Adok, therefore, consisted merely of running, jumping, and climbing over various obstacles, with the enablers assisting. After the first session of this exercise, which Adok permitted to go on only for some twelve minutes, the Starkien took Jim almost tenderly back to his own quarters and had Jim lie down on the oversized hassock that served as a bed there, while Adok gently removed the class-two weaponry bands.

"Now," said Adok, "you must rest for at least three hours."

"Why?" Jim asked, curiously gazing up at the stocky figure standing over him.

"Because the first effects of wearing the enablers is not appreciated by the body immediately," said Adok. "Remember, your muscles have been forced to move faster than your nature intended them to. You may think that you feel stiff and sore now. But what you feel now is nothing to what you will feel in about three hours' time. The best way of minimizing the stiffness and soreness when you first begin to use the enablers is to remain as still as possible for the three hours immediately following exercise. As you become hardened to their use, your body will actually adapt to being pushed at faster than its normal speed of reflex. Eventually you won't become stiff unless you really overextend yourself, and you won't need to rest after each exercise."

Jim kept his face impassive, and Adok vanished, considerately dimming the lights of the room before he went. In the dimness Jim looked thoughtfully at the white ceiling overhead.

He felt no stiffness or soreness of his muscles whatever. But, as Adok had said, possibly the maximum effect would not be appreciated until about three hours from now. Conscientiously, therefore, he waited those three hours without moving from the bed.

But at the end of that time, he found no difference in himself. He was not sore, and he was not stiff. He filed that piece of information with the gradually accumulating store of knowledge about the Throne World and its inhabitants in the back of his mind.

It did not immediately fit with the other pieces of the jigsaw puzzle that was forming in his mind. But one of the things that had helped him, from that day when as a boy he had at last faced the fact that he had no choice but to bear the loneliness of his life in silence, was the capacity in him for an almost infinite patience. The picture forming in his mind was not yet readable. But it would be. Until then . . . Adok had assumed that at the end of three hours the stiffness and soreness of Jim's body would have effectively immobilized him. Since he had never been able to discover if he might be under surveillance—and to this he had added lately the possibility of surveillance not only by High-born, for their own reasons, but also by servants, for *their* own reasons—he resigned himself to staying as he was.

Stretched out on his hassocklike bed, he willed himself to sleep

When he woke up, it was because Ro was shaking him gently. She stood in the dimness of the room beside his bed.

"There's someone Galyan wants you to meet," she said. "He sent word through Afuan. It's the Governor of the Colony Worlds of Alpha Centauri."

He blinked at her for a moment sleepily. Then wakefulness sprang upon him, as the implications of what she had said woke inside him.

"Why would I want to meet the Governor of the worlds of Alpha Centauri?" he asked, sitting abruptly upon the hassock-bed.

"But he's *your* Governor!" Ro said. "Didn't anyone ever tell you, Jim? Any new Colony World is first assigned to the nearest Governor."

"No," said Jim, swinging his legs over the edge of the bed and getting to his feet. "No one ever did tell me. Does this mean I have some sort of obligation to this Governor?"

"Well . . ." Ro hesitated. "In theory, he

can take you away from the Throne World right now, since you're under his authority. But, on the other hand, the sponsorship for your adoption has been entered. In practice, he would find this out and would know better than to try to do anything that might interfere with any possible future Highborn. Remember, his worlds will gain a lot of prestige if anyone under their authority becomes at least a probationary High-born. In other words, he can't really do you any harm; but you can hardly, politely, turn down the chance to visit with him, now that he's here."

"I see," said Jim grimly. "They sent you to bring me?"

Ro nodded. He reached out his hand, and she took it in one of hers. It was an easy, shorthand way of taking somebody else where they had never been before. It required a certain mental effort, Jim had been told, to transport someone to a place unknown to him but known to his guide, without this physical contact. Adok, of course, as with Ro earlier, had done it the polite way. But now Ro customarily reached out and took hold of him when she wished to take him anyplace.

Immediately they were in a relatively small room—a room, however, which in the number of writing surfaces standing flatly suspended in midair, and the relative scarcity of sitting hassocks, bespoke the utilitarian kind of office-type room that Galyan had brought Jim to aboard the ship.

Present in the room were the usual workers and the single Starkien bodyguard. Present also was Galyan, and with him a man with the American Indian-like coloring of the Alpha Centaurans. But this man was almost five-ten, a good three or four inches taller than most of the Alpha Centaurans Jim had met when he had been on Alpha Centauri III.

"There you are, Jim—and you too, Ro," said Galyan, turning softly to face them as they appeared. "Jim, I thought you might like to meet your regional overlord—Wyk Ben of Alpha Centauri III. Wyk Ben, this is Jim Keil, sponsorship of whom has been offered here on the Throne World."

"Yeth," agreed Wyk Ben, turning quickly to face Jim and smiling. In contrast to the hissing accent of the High-born, which had come to sound almost natural to Jim by this time, the Governor of Alpha Centauri lisped slightly in his speech.

"I just wanted to see you for a moment, Jim, to wish you luck. Here, your world's just come under our Governorship . . . and, well, I'm very proud!"

Wky Ben smiled happily at Jim, apparently unaware that of the three other people concerned in the conversation, there was a slight frown of foreboding on the face of Ro, a touch of sardonic humor in the lemon-yellow eyes of Galyan, and a detachment and reserve about Jim.

"Well . . . I just wanted to tell you. I won't take up any more of your time," said Wyk Ben eagerly.

Jim stared down at him. He was absurdly like a puppy wagging its tail in eagerness and pride, coupled with a sort of innocence about the Throne World in general. Jim could not understand why Galyan should have wanted him to meet this man. But he filed the fact that Galyan *had* wanted him to meet the Alpha Centauran Governor, for future reference.

"Thank you again," Jim said. "Yes, as a matter of fact, I'm due for an exercise session with the Starkien who's my substitute." He looked over at Ro. "Ro?"

"Good to have seen you again, Jim," said Galyan slowly in a tone of voice almost matching the amused drawl of Slothiel. Clearly, whatever he had hoped to gain from bringing Jim and Wyk Ben face to face, he had gained. But there was no point in trying to pursue the matter, here and now, any further. Jim turned to Ro and held out his hand. She took it, and immediately they were back in his room.

"What was all that about?" asked Jim.

Ro shook her head puzzledly.

"I don't know," she said not happily. "And when anything happens on the Throne World that you don't understand, it's a danger signal. I'll try to find out, Jim—I'll see you later."

Hastily she disappeared.

Left by himself, Jim ran over the meeting with Wyk Ben in his mind. It struck him that things were in danger of happening so fast that they might get ahead of him. He spoke out loud to the empty room.

"Adok!"

It took possibly three seconds—no more— and then the figure of the Starkien appeared before him.

"How are you feeling?" asked Adok. "Do you need—"

"Nothing," said Jim brusquely. "Adok, are there any library facilities down in the servant's area, underground?"

"Library? . . ." For a moment Adok's face squeezed faintly, in what Jim was beginning to understand was an expression of extreme puzzlement. Then it cleared. "Oh, of course, you mean a learning center. Yes, I'll take you to one, Jim. I've never been there myself, but I know about where it is."

Adok ventured to touch Jim on the arm, and they were in the underground park Jim had passed through with Adok before. Adok hesitated, then turned left and began to walk off toward a side street.

"This way, I think," he said. Jim followed him, and they left the park, going down the street until they came to a flight of what looked like wide stone steps leading up to a tall open portal in a wall of polished brown stone.

There were a few people coming and going through the portal, up and down the steps—all of them servants rather than Starkiens. Jim watched these, as he had watched all the servants they had passed on the way here, with a close attention. Now, going up the steps, his concentration was rewarded. Coming out of the portal as he and Adok started up the steps was a yellowish-skinned, black-eyed man like Melness. As he started down the steps, his eyes went to one of the servants entering—one of the short brown men with long, straight hair. The brown man ran the heel of his hand, in apparently an idle gesture, across his waist just at belt level. In response, without breaking stride, the yellow-skinned man who looked like Melness reached casually across with his right hand to lay two fingers momentarily against the biceps of his left arm, before dropping the arm once more to his side.

Without another gesture—in fact, without looking at each other after that—the two passed, going opposite ways on the steps.

"Did you see that?" Jim asked in a low voice to Adok as they entered the portal. "Those gestures? What were they all about?"

For an unusually long moment Adok did not answer, so that Jim turned to glance at him as they walked. Adok's face, insofar as Jim could read it, was serious.

"It's strange," said the Starkien, almost

to himself. "There *has* been more of it lately."

He lifted his eyes to Jim.

"It's their Silent Language."

"What did they say, then?" asked Jim. Adok shook his head."

"I don't know," he answered. "It's an old language—the High-born first learned of it after the first Servant's Revolt, thousands of years ago. The servants have always used it. But we Starkiens are shut out from it. That's because we're always loyal to the Emperor."

"I see," said Jim. He became thoughtful.

They passed down a wide hallway of the same polished brown stone and into a large interior room which seemed brown stone and into a large interior room which seemed to be filled with rank on rank of whirling, glowing globes of light—like small suns. They spun—if that indeed was what they were doing—too fast for the eye to follow their rotation. But they were obviously in constant movement.

Adok halted. He gestured at the miniature suns.

"This is one of the Files," he said. "Which one, I don't know, because they're designed to feed not to us here but to the learning centers for the young High-born above ground. But off to the right here there're carrels, where you can tap the information stored, not only here, but in Files all over the Throne World."

He led Jim off to the right and out of the room with the miniature suns into a long, narrow corridor with a series of open doorways running down its right side. Adok led him down the corridor and into one of the doorways.

Within was a small room—the first unoccupied one they had passed—fitted with a chair and a sort of desk or table, with a raised surface, sloping upward at an angle of about forty-five degrees to the horizontal.

Jim sat down in front of the raised surface, which seemed perfectly blank except for a pair of small black studs, or buttons, near the bottom. Adok reached over and touched one of the buttons, however, and immediately the sloping surface resolved itself into a white screen, with one word, in the sort of shorthand figures that were the Imperial language, glowing blackly in the center of it. The word was "ready."

"Speak to it," said Adok.

"I'd like to examine whatever records there are of Empire expeditions," said Jim slowly to the screen, "with a view to finding any that went out past—" and he gave the Imperial name for Alpha Centauri.

The squiggles that stood for the Imperial word "ready" vanished from the screen. Its place was taken by a line of writing moving from left to right at a slow pace.

Jim sat, reading. It appeared that the retrieval system of the File was not equipped to hunt down the information he wanted directly. It could only supply him with a vast quantity of information about past expeditions in general out in the direction in which Alpha Centauri lay from the Throne World. Apparently Jim's task would require his searching all the relevant records of expeditions in that general direction in order to find the one which had gone on to Earth—if indeed any expedition ever had. It was not a task to be done at one sitting, Jim saw. It would take hours, days, perhaps even weeks.

"Is there any way to speed this up?" he asked, looking up at Adok. Adok reached over to the second stud and turned it. The line of type moving across the screen began to move more rapidly. Adok's hand fell away, and Jim raised his own. He continued to increase the speed of the line until the stud stopped, evidently having reached its highest rate. Adok made a small sound, like a badly stifled grunt of surprise.

"What?" demanded Jim, not lifting his eyes from the swiftly sliding line of information.

"You read," said Adok, "almost like a High-born."

Jim did not bother to answer that. He remained fixed before the screen, hardly conscious that time was sliding by, until, with the ending of one set of records and the beginning of the next, there was a momentary interruption in which he became conscious of the fact that he had very nearly stiffened in position, after sitting without moving for so long.

He straightened up, shut off the machine for a moment, and looked about him. Abruptly, he saw Adok, still standing beside him. Evidently the Starkien had not moved either.

"Have you been waiting there all this time?" asked Jim. "How long have I been reading?"

"Some little time," said Adok without apparent emotion. He gave Jim a period in Empire time units that was the equivalent of a little over four hours.

Jim shook his head and got to his feet. Then, remembering, he sat down before the screen again and turned it on. He asked for information on the Silent Language.

The screen responded—not with one Silent Language, but with fifty-two of them. Apparently there had been fifty-two recorded "revolts" by the servants of the Throne World. Jim made a mental note to look up these revolts next time he was here. Apparently, after each revolt the High-born had investigated and translated the secrets of the current Silent Language; but by the time the next revolt took place, some hundreds or thousands of years later, an entirely new language had grown up.

They were not so much languages, in fact, as sets of signals—like the signals passed back and forth between the pitcher and the catcher in a baseball game, or between the players in the game and the coaches on the

sideline. Rubbing one's fingers together, or
scratching one's chin, was clearly and visibly a signal—or a part of the current Silent
Language. The question lay not in seeing
the signal but in interpreting it. The question was what it meant this particular time.

Jim skimmed the information of the Silent Languages, shut off the machine, and
got to his feet. He and Adok left the Files,
and with Jim leading, they walked out of
the place, down the steps, and back into the
community area near the park.

They strolled about its streets, shops, and
places of entertainment for nearly an hour,
while Jim kept his eyes quietly alert for any
more signals in the current Silent Language.

He saw many, none of which made sense
according to any of the earlier fifty-two ver-
sions of the language. Nonetheless, he carefully stored up in his memory each signal
as he saw it, and the conditions under which
it was used. After a certain time of this, he
left Adok and returned to his own room.

He had hardly been back five minutes
when Ro appeared, accompanied by Slothiel.
Jim made a mental note to ask Ro what
kind of warning system alerted her that he
was back in his quarters, and also how such
a warning system could be screened out or
turned off.

But as he rose to face the two of them
now, he mentally filed that thought also, at
the sight of the faint worry on the face of

Ro and the look of rather grim humor on Slothiel's face.

"I take it something's happened?" Jim asked.

"You take it correctly," answered Slothiel. "Your adoption is being approved, and Galyan has just now suggested to me that I give a large party for you to celebrate. I didn't realize he was that much a friend of yours. Now, why do you suppose he'd do something like that?"

"If you give such a party," said Jim, "will the Emperor attend?"

"The Emperor and Vhotan," answered Slothiel. "Yes, almost certainly they'll both be there. Why?"

"Because," said Jim, "that's why Galyan suggested you give the party."

Slothiel frowned. It was a slightly haughty frown, with the faint implication that a member of the lesser races should not make statements to a High-born that a High-born could not fully understand.

"Why do you say that?" asked Slothiel.

"Because Melness is a very clever man," said Jim.

Chapter 7

Slothiel's tall body stiffened.

"All right, Wolfling!" he snapped. "We've had enough question-and-answer games!"

"Jim—" began Ro warningly.

"I'm sorry," said Jim, looking steadily at the taller man. "The explanation doesn't concern me—it concerns the Emperor. So I'm not going to give it to you. And you're not going to force me to give it. In the first place, you can't. And in the second place, it would be impolitic of you to try, since you're the one who's sponsoring me for adoption."

Slothiel stood perfectly still.

"Believe me," said Jim, this time persuasively, "if I was free to answer you, I would. Let me make you a promise. If by the time the party is over you haven't had an assurance either from the Emperor or from Vhotan that I had good reason not to tell you, then I'll answer any question you have about the whole thing. All right?"

For a long second longer Slothiel remained rigid, his eyes burning down at Jim. Then, abruptly, the tension leaked out of him, and he smiled his old, lazy smile.

"You know, you have me there, Jim," he drawled. "I can hardly forcibly question the very lesser human I'm sponsoring for adoption, can I? Particularly since it would be impossible to keep the fact quiet. You'll make a good man at wagering for points, if by some freak chance you ever should happen to get adopted, Jim. All right, keep your secret—for now."

He disappeared.

"Jim," said Ro, "I worry about you."

For some reason, the words rang with unusual importance in his mind. He looked about at her sharply and saw why they had. She was looking at him with concern, but it was a different sort of concern from that which she lavished on all her pets and which she had heretofore lavished on him. And the tone of her voice had conveyed a difference to match.

He was suddenly, unexpectedly, and deeply touched. No one, man or woman, had worried about him for a very very long time.

"Can't you at least tell *me* why you say Galyan's suggesting the party because Melness is a very clever man? Ro asked. "It sounds as if you're saying that there's some connection between Galyan and Melness. But that can't be between a High-born and one of the lesser races."

"How about you and me," said Jim, remembering that new note in her voice.

She blushed, but this, as he had come to learn, did not mean as much with her as it might have with another woman.

"I'm different!" she said. "But Galyan isn't. He's one of the highest of High-born. Not just by birth—by attitude, too."

"But he's always made it a point to make a good deal of use of men of the lesser races."

"That's true. . . ." She became thoughtful. Then she looked back up at him. "But you still haven't explained. . . ."

"There's nothing much to explain," said Jim, "except for that part that I say is really a matter belonging to the Emperor rather than to me. I said what I did about Melness being a clever man because men can make mistakes out of their own cleverness, as well as out of foolishness. They can try too hard to cover something up. In Melness' case, when Adok first took me to meet him, Melness went to a great deal of trouble to make it look as if he resented my being placed under his responsibility."

Ro frowned.

"But why should he resent . . ."

"There could be a number of reasons, of course," said Jim. "For one—and the easiest answer—the fact that he resented a Wolfling like myself being sponsored for adoption when a man like him stands no chance of such sponsorship, just because he is so useful in his capacity as a servant. But, by the same token, Melness should have been too clever to let me know that resentment, particularly when there was a possibility that I might end up as a High-born myself, in a position to resent him in return."

"They why did he do it?" asked Ro.

"Possibly because he thought I might be a spy sent by the High-born to investigate the world of servants," said Jim, "and he wanted to set up a reason for harassing or observing me while I was underground that would not lead me to suspect that he suspected I was a spy."

"But what would you be spying on him for?" asked Ro.

"That, I don't know yet," said Jim.

"But you think it has something to do with the Emperor and with Galyan. Why?" Ro said.

Jim smiled down at her.

"You want to know too much too quickly," he said. "In fact, you want to know more than I know yet. You see why I didn't want to get into questions and answers on this with Slothiel?"

Slowly she nodded. Then she gazed at him with concern again.

"Jim—" she said unexpectedly. "What did you do? I mean, besides bullfighting, when you were back on your own world among your own people?"

"I was an anthropologist," he told her. "Bullfighting was—a late avocation with me."

She frowned puzzeldly. For to his knowledge, the word did not exist in the Empire tongue, and so he had simply translated it literally from the Latin root—"man-science."

"I studied the primitive background of man," said Jim. "Particularly the roots of culture—all cultures—in the basic nature of humankind."

He could almost see the lightning search she was making through that massive Highborn memory of hers. Her face lit up.

"Oh, you mean—*anthropology!*" She gave him the Empire word he had needed. Then her face softened, and she touched his arm. "Jim! Poor Jim—no wonder!"

Once again—as he so often found it necessary to do—he had to restrain the impulse to smile at her. He had thought of himself in many terms during his lifetime so far. But to date he had never had occasion to think of himself as "poor"—in any sense of the word.

"No wonder?" he echoed.

"I mean, no wonder you always seem so cold and distant to anyone High-born," she said. "Oh, I don't mean me! I mean the others. But, no wonder you're that way. Finding out about us and the Empire put an end to everything you'd studied, didn't it? You had to face the fact that you weren't evolved from the ape-men and prehumans of your own world. It meant all the work you'd ever done had to be thrown out."

"Not exactly," said Jim.

"Jim, let me tell you something," she said;

"the same thing happened to us, you know. I mean us—the High-born. Some thousands of years ago the early High-born used to think that they were evolved from the prehumans on this one Throne World. But finally they had to admit that not even that was true. The animal forms were too much the same on all the worlds like this one that our people settled. Finally, even we had to face the fact that all these worlds had evidently been stocked with the common ancestors of their present flora and fauna by some intelligent race that existed even long before our time. And the evidence is pretty overwhelming that the ancestors with which this world was stocked were probably a strain pointing toward a superior type of premen then were planted elsewhere. So, you see, we had to face the fact that we weren't the first thinking beings in the universe, too."

This time Jim let himself smile.

"Don't worry," he told her. "Whatever shock there was to me on learning the Empire existed has evaporated by this time."

She was, he thought, reassured.

The party celebrating Slothiel's sponsorhip of him for adoption, it turned out, was to be held in just under three weeks. Jim spent the time learning Starkien ways and warfare from Adok, putting in the few nominal appearances that duty required of him with that military caste and studying in the Files section to which Adok had introduced him underground.

In between times, he moved about the servants' areas underground, observing any hand signal that was made and committing it to memory. In his spare time he tried to catalog and arrange these signals into some kind of coherent form that would allow him to begin to interpret them.

Two things were in his favor. In the first place, as an anthropologist, he was aware that any sign language derived from primitive, common basics in human nature. As one of the early explorers had said about his experiences in that regard while living with the North American Eskimo, you did not need anyone to teach you the basic signs of communication. You already knew them. The threatening gesture; the come-here gesture; the I-am-hungry gestures, such as pointing to the mouth and then rubbing the stomach—all these, and a large handful more, came instinctively to the mind of any man trying to communicate by hand or body movements.

In the second place, a language mainly of hand signals was necessarily limited. The messages conveyed by such a language necessarily had to depend a great deal upon the context in which the gestures were made. Therefore, the same signal was bound to reappear frequently before any observer watching over a period of time.

Jim therefore assumed success. And, in

fact, it was only a little more than two weeks
before he identified the recognition signal—
that hand movement that was equivalent to
a greeting and a recognition signal among
users of the Silent Language. It consisted of
nothing more than the tapping of the right
thumbtip against the side of the adjacent
forefinger. From that point on, the various
signals began to reveal their meaning to
him rapidly.

His search in the Files to discover whether
an expedition from the Throne World—or,
for that matter, from one of the then-existing
Colony Worlds—had set out in the direction
of the solar system containing Earth was
meeting with no similar success. Perhaps
records of such an expedition were there
in the Files. Perhaps they were not. The
point was, the records that Jim himself
had to examine to eliminate all the possibili-
ties were too multitudinous. The job was
equivalent, in fact, to his reading through
the entire contents of a small public library.

"And besides," said Adok when Jim finally one day mentioned this problem to
the Starkien, "you have to remember that
you could go all through the records you're
permitted to see and still not know of such
an expedition, even if record of it was there."

They had been strolling through the underground park. Jim stopped suddenly and
turned to face Adok, who automatically
stopped also and turned to face Jim.

"What's this?" demanded Jim. "You said

something about my being permitted to see
only part of the records?"

"Forgive me, Jim," said Adok. "I don't
know, of course, if any of the records of
such trips are secret. But the point is, how
can you be sure some are not? And further,
how can you be sure that if some are secret,
the one you're looking for is not among
them?"

"I can't. Naturally," said Jim. "What both-
ers me is that I never stopped to think that
any of the history of this planet might not
be fully available." He thought for a second.
"Who gets to see secret information in the
Files, anyway?"

"Why," answered Adok with the faint note
of surprise in his voice that was the ultimate in his reaction that way, "all the High-
born see all the information, of course. In
fact, since you are as free to move around
above ground as below, all you need to do
is to go to one of the learning centers for
the High-born children—"

He broke off suddenly.

"No," he said in a lower tone of voice. "I
was forgetting. You can go to one of the
learning centers, of course. But it won't do
you any good."

"You mean the High-born won't let me
use the learning center?" asked Jim. He was
watching Adok closely. Nothing on the
Throne World could be taken for granted,
even the transparent honesty in someone
like Adok. If Adok was going to tell him

that there was some kind of a rule against his using the learning center, it would be only the second outright prohibition he had encountered above ground on this singularly prohibitionless planet. The first, of course, being the rule against anyone approaching the Emperor without being directly summoned. But Adok was shaking his head.

"No," Adok said. "I don't think anyone would stop you. It's just that you wouldn't be able to use the reading machines above ground. You see, they're set for use by the young High-born, and they read too fast for the ordinary men to follow."

"You've seen me read," said Jim. "They read faster than that?"

"Much faster," said Adok. He shook his head again. "Much, much faster."

"That's all right," said Jim. "Take me to one of these learning centers."

Adok did not shrug—in fact, it was a question whether his shoulders were not too heavily muscled for such a gesture, even if his nature permitted it. Instantly they were above ground in a large structure like an enormous loggia—or rather, like one of the Grecian temples, consisting of roof and pillars and floor, but without any obvious outside walls. Through the nearby pillars green lawn and blue sky showed. About on the floor, scattered at intervals, seated or curled up on hassocks, were children obviously of the High-born, and of all ages. Each of them was gazing at a screen that floated at an angle in the air before them, and moved about to stay before them as they altered position on the hassock, always maintaining roughly the same forty-five-degree reading angle Jim had found in the carrels of the Files below ground.

None of the children, even the few who paused to glance at Jim and Adok, paid more than a second's attention to the newcomers. Clearly, Jim decided, the fact that neither he nor Adok was a High-born rendered them for practical purposes invisible, unless needed, by these High-born children.

Jim moved over to stand closely behind one of them—a boy as tall as Jim himself, though extremely thin of limb and with the face of a ten- or twelve-year-old. The same running line of symbols to which Jim had grown accustomed below ground was running in front of the youngster. Jim looked at that line.

It was blurring by at a tremendous rate. Jim frowned, staring at it, trying to match his perception to its movement, to change it from a streak of spiky, wavy blackness to readable symbols.

Astonishingly, he could not.

He felt a sudden shock through him internally of something very like anger. He had never yet found anything that anyone else could do that he was not capable of matching within the limits of his own physical resources. Moreover, he was perfectly sure that the problem was not with his vision. His eyes should be as capable of resolving the blurred line into symbols as any High-born eye. The problem was in his brain, which was refusing to accept the readable information at the rate at which it was being offered.

He made a grim internal effort. Around him, glimpses of sunlight and lawn, pillars, ceiling, floor—even the boy himself, unheed-ingly reading—were blanked out. Jim's concentration focused down upon the line of reading—the line alone. The pressure of his efforts to resolve it was like a cord twisted tight around the temples of his head. Tighter, and tighter. . . .

Almost, for a second, he made it. For a second it seemed as if the line was beginning to break apart into readable symbols, and he gathered that the text had something to do with the organization of the Starkiens themselves. Then his efforts broke—out of sheer physical inability of his body to sustain it any longer. He swayed a little, and vision of the rest of the universe, including pillars, walls, and ceiling, opened out about him once more.

He was suddenly aware that the boy on the hassock had noticed him finally. The High-born child had stopped reading and was staring at Jim himself with a plain expression of astonishment.

"Who are you—?" the boy began in a reedy voice. But Jim, without answering, touched Adok on the arm and translated them both back to Jim's quarters before the question could be completed.

Back in the familiar room, Jim breathed deeply for a second and then sat down on one of the hassocks. He motioned Adok to sit down likewise, and the Starkien obeyed. After a moment Jim's deep breathing slowed, and he smiled slightly. He looked across at Adok.

"You don't say, 'I told you so!' " said Jim.

Adok shook his head in a gesture that clearly conveyed that it was not his place to say such things.

"Well, you were right," said Jim. He became thoughtful. "But not for the reasons you think. What stopped me just then was the fact that I hadn't been born to this language of yours. If that writing had been in my own native tongue, I could've read it."

He turned his head abruptly away from Adok and spoke to the empty air.

"Ro?" he asked.

He and Adok both waited. But there was no answer, and Ro did not materialize. This was not surprising. Ro was a High-born and had her own occupations and duties, unlike Adok, whose single duty was to await, and wait upon, Jim's call.

Jim shifted himself to Ro's apartment, found it empty, and left a note asking her to contact him as soon as she came in. It was about two and a half hours later that she suddenly appeared beside Adok and him in the main room of Jim's quarters.

"It's going to be a big party," she said without preamble. "Everybody's going to be there. They'll have to use the Great Gathering Room. The word must've gotten out somehow that there's something special about this celebration—" She broke off suddenly. "I'm forgetting. You wanted to see me about something, Jim?"

"Oh," said Jim, "could you get one of those reading screens from the learning centers set up in your apartment?"

"Why—of course!" said Ro. "Do you want to use one, Jim? Why don't I just have one set up for you here?"

Jim shook his head.

"I'd rather not have it generally known that I was using it," Jim said. "I take it that it isn't too unusual a thing for someone like you to want one where she lives?"

"Not unusual. No. . . ." said Ro. "And of course if you want it that way, that's the way I can do it. But what's this all about?"

Jim told her about his attempt to try to read at the same speed as that of the young High-born he had stood behind in the learning center.

"You think study will speed up your reading comprehension?" asked Ro. She frowned. "Maybe you shouldn't get your hopes too high—"

"I won't," said Jim.

Within a few hours the screen was set up,

floating in a corner of one of the less-used rooms of Ro's apartment. From then on, Jim spent the time he had spent in the Files underground in Ro's apartment room instead.

He had made only slight progress, however, within the next week. He gave it up entirely and spent the last few days before the party lounging around the underground servants' area with Adok, observing the Silent Language in use about him. He had become fluent in understanding it now, but, wearyingly, most of what he absorbed was the hand-signaled equivalent of gossip. Nonetheless, gossip could be useful if properly sifted and interpreted.

Jim returned from the last of these expeditions just an hour or so before the party, to find Lorava waiting for him in the main room of his quarters.

"Vhotan wants to see you," said Lorava abruptly as Jim appeared.

No more notice than that. Jim found himself standing beside Lorava in a room he had not been in before. Adok was on the other side of him, so evidently the invitation had included the Starkien as well.

Vhotan was seated on a hassock before a flat surface suspended in midair with its top covered with what looked like several different studs of various shapes and colors. He was turning or depressing these studs in what appeared to be a random pattern, but with a seriousness and intensity that suggested his actions were far from unimportant. Nonetheless, he broke off at the sight of them, rose from his hassock, and came over to face Jim.

"I'll call for you a little later, Lorava!" he said.

The thin young High-born vanished.

"Wolfling," said Vhotan to Jim, his yellowish brows drawing together, "the Emperor is going to attend this party of yours."

"I don't believe it's my party," answered Jim. "I think it's Slothiel's party."

Vhotan brushed the objection aside with a short wave of one long hand.

"You're the reason for it," he said. "And you're the reason for the Emperor being at it. He wants to talk to you again."

"Naturally," said Jim. "I can come anytime the Emperor wants to summon me. It needn't be at the party."

"He's at his best in public!" said Vhotan sharply. "Never mind that. The point is, at the party the Emperor will want to talk to you. He'll take you off to one side and undoubtedly ask you a lot of questions."

Vhotan hesitated.

"I'll be glad to answer any of the Emperor's questions," said Jim.

"Yes . . . you do exactly that," said Vhotan gruffly. "Whatever questions he asks you, answer them fully. You understand? He's the Emperor, and even if he doesn't seem to be paying you complete attention, I want you to go right on answering until he asks

you another question or tells you to stop.
Do you understand?"

"Fully," said Jim. His eyes met the lemon-
yellow eyes of the older, High-born man.

"Yes. Well," said Vhotan, turning abruptly,
walking back to his console of studs, and
sitting down before it once again.

"That's all. You can go back to your quarters now."

His fingers began to move over the studs.
Jim touched Adok on the arm and shifted
back to the main room of his own apartment.

"What do you make of that?" he asked
Adok.

"Make of it?" Adok repeated slowly.

"Yes," said Jim. He eyed the Starkien
keenly. "Didn't you think that some of what
he said was a little strange?"

Adok's face was completely without expression.

"Nothing dealing with the Emperor can be
strange," he said. His voice was strangely
remote. "The High-born Vhotan told you to
answer fully to the questions of the Emperor.
That is all. There could not be any more
than that."

"Yes," said Jim. "Adok, you've been lent
to me to be my substitute. But you still
belong to the Emperor, don't you?"

"As I told you, Jim," said Adok, still in
the same expressionless, remote voice. "All
Starkiens always belong to the Emperor, no
matter where they are or what they're
doing."

"I remember," said Jim.

He turned away and went to get out of the Starkien straps and belts he had been wearing, into the white costume like that of all the male High-born, but without insignia, which he had chosen to wear for the occasion.

He was barely dressed when Ro appeared. In fact, she materialized so suspiciously close upon the end of his dressing that once more he wondered whether he was not under surveillance—by others as well as Ro—more than he thought. But he had no chance to speculate upon this now.

"Here," she said a little breathlessly, "put this on."

He saw she was holding out to him what seemed to be something like a narrow band of white satin. When he hesitated, she picked up his left arm and wrapped it around his wrist, without waiting for his approval.

"Now," she said, "touch mine." She held up her own left wrist, around which was already wrapped—and clinging as if through some inner life of its own—a similar piece of white cloth. It was the only piece of clothlike material that she was wearing. Otherwise, she was clothed from shoulders to ankles in that same filmy, cloudlike stuff that he had seen Afuan and the other High-born women wearing at the bullfight on Alpha Centauri III.

She picked Jim's wrist up and touched his band to hers.

"What's this?" asked Jim.

"Oh—of course you don't know," she said. "At a party, particularly a big one like this, people move around so much that you can't keep track of where someone is if you want to find them. But now that we've checked our sensors with each other, all you have to do is visualize me, and you'll automatically come to whatever part of the Great Gathering Room I'm in. You'll see." She laughed a little. To his surprise, she was more than a little bright-eyed and excited. "Everything's always very mixed up on occasions like this!"

When they, with Adok, moved to the Great Gathering Room forty minutes or so later, Jim immediately saw what she had meant. The Great Gathering Room was a wall-less, pillared, and roofed area like the learning center he had visited, only much larger. Clearly its polished floor of utter black, upon which the white pillars seemed to float, was at least several square miles in area. On that floor groups of male and female High-born, in their usual white costume, stood talking, while servants moved among them carrying trays of various edibles and drinkables.

At first sight, except for the appearance of the High-born and the size of it all, the gathering looked ordinary enough. But as he gazed, Jim became aware that not only High-born individuals themselves, but the servants, were appearing and disappearing continuously all over the place. For a moment, even to Jim, the size and movement of the crowd was slightly dizzying.

Then he did what he had always done when faced with a situation that threatened a temporary mental or emotional overload. He filed what he could not handle in the back of his mind and concentrated on what he could.

"Adok," he said, turning to the Starkien, "I want you to circulate. Try to locate for me a particular servant. I don't know what he'll look like, but he'll be a little different from all the rest, in that he will, first, have a fixed position in the room someplace; second, it will be a fairly secluded position, from which only one other servant in the hall at any time will be able to see him. He may be watched by any number of other servants in succession, but there will never be more than one watching him at a time, and he will always be under surveillance by the other servant observing him at the time. Will you get busy about that right away?"

"Yes, Jim," said Adok. He vanished.

"Why did you ask him to do that?" asked Ro in a low, puzzled voice, pressing close to him.

"I'll tell you later," said Jim.

He saw by her attitude that she would like to ask him more questions, in spite of this answer of his. She might indeed have done so, but at that moment Vhotan and the Emperor appeared beside them.

"There he is—my Wolfling!" said the Em-

peror cheerfully. "Come and talk to me,
Wolfling!"

Instantly, with his words, Ro vanished.
Also, all the other High-born nearby began
to disappear, until Jim, Vhotan, and the
Emperor were surrounded by an open space
perhaps fifty feet in diameter, within which
they could talk in casual tones without anyone else being near enough to overhear. The
Emperor turned his gaze on the older High-
born.

"Go on," he said, "enjoy yourself for once,
Vhotan. I'll be all right."

Vhotan hesitated a moment, then winked
out of sight.

The Emperor turned back to Jim.

"I like you—what is your name, Wolfling?"
he asked.

"Jim, Oran," answered Jim.

"I like you, Jim." The Emperor leaned
down, stooping a little from his more than
seven feet of height, and laid a long hand
on Jim's shoulder, resting part of his weight
on Jim like a tired man. Slowly he began to
pace idly up and down. Jim kept level with
him, held by the shoulder.

"It's a wild world you come from, Jim?"
Oran asked.

"Up until about half a century ago," said
Jim. "Very wild."

They had gone perhaps half a dozen steps
in one direction. The Emperor turned them
about, and they began to pace back again.
All the while they talked, they continued

this movement—half a dozen paces one way, half a dozen paces back again, turn and return.

"You mean, in only fifty years you people tamed this world of yours?" asked the Emperor.

"No, Oran," said Jim. "We tamed the world sometime before that. It's just that fifty years ago we finally succeeded in taming ourselves."

Oran nodded, his gaze not on Jim, but fixed on the floor a little ahead of them as they moved.

"Yes, that's the human part of it. The self-taming is always the hardest," he said, almost as if to himself. "You know, my cousin Galyan, looking at you, would think immediately, what marvelous servants these people would make. And perhaps he's right. Perhaps he's right ... but"—they turned about at the end of one of their short distances of pacing, and the Emperor for a moment looked from the floor up and over at Jim with a friendly smile—"I don't think so. We've had too many servants."

The smile faded. For a moment they paced in silence.

"You have your own language?" murmured the Emperor in Jim's ear, once more gazing at the floor as they went. "Your own art and music and history and legend?"

"Yes, Oran," said Jim.

"Then you deserve better than to be servants. At least"—once more the Emperor flashed one of his quick, brief, friendly smiles at Jim before returning his eyes to the floor ahead of them—"I know that you, at least, deserve better. You know, I shouldn't be surprised if someday I really do approve your adoption, so that you become technically one of us."

Jim said nothing. After a second, and after they had completed another turn, the Emperor looked sideways at him.

"Would you like that, Jim?" Oran said.

"I don't know yet, Oran," said Jim.

"An honest answer ..." murmured the Emperor. "An honest answer ... You know how they tell us, Jim, in probability, all events must sooner or later occur?"

"In probability?" Jim asked. But the Emperor went on as if he had not heard.

"Somewhere," said the Emperor, "there must be a probability in which you, Jim, were the Emperor, and all the people of your world were High-born. And I was a Wolfling, who was brought there to show off some barbaric skill to you and your court. ..."

The grip on Jim's shoulder had tightened. Glancing up and sideways, Jim saw that the Emperor's eyes had become abstracted and seemingly out of focus. Though he continued to push Jim forward with his grip on Jim's shoulder, it was now as if he were blind and letting Jim find the path for him, so that he followed Jim, instead of leading him, as he had at the beginning of their pacing.

"Have you ever heard of a Blue Beast, Jim?" he murmured.

"No, Oran," said Jim.

"No. . . ." muttered the Emperor. "No, and neither have I. Also, I looked through all our records of all the human legends on all the worlds—and nowhere was there a Blue Beast. If there never was such a thing as a Blue Beast, why should I see one, Jim?"

The grip on Jim's shoulder was like a vice now. Still, the Emperor's voice was murmurous and soft, almost idle, as if he were daydreaming out loud. To any of the Highborn watching from the edges of the circle surrounding them, it must look as if the two of them were in perfectly sensible, though low-voiced conversation.

"I don't know, Oran," answered Jim.

"Neither do I, Jim," said the Emperor. "That's what makes it so strange. Three times I've seen it now, and always in a doorway ahead of me, as if it was barring my path. You know, Jim . . . sometimes I'm just like all the rest of the High-born. But there are other times in which my mind becomes very clear . . . and I see things, and understand them, much better than any of these around us. That's why I know you're different, Jim. When I first saw you after the bullfight, I was looking at you . . . and all of a sudden it was as if you were at the other end of the telescope—very small, but

very sharp. And I saw many very small,
very sharp details about you that none of
the rest of us had seen. You can be a High-
born or not, Jim. Just as you like. Because it
doesn't matter ... I saw that in you. It
doesn't matter."

The Emperor's voice stopped. But he continued to urge Jim on, pacing blindly alongside him.

"That's the way it is with me, Jim ..."
he began again after a moment. "Sometimes
I see things small and clear. Then I realize
that I'm half a step beyond the rest of the
High-born. And it's strange—I'm what we've
been working for down all these generations—that one step further on. But it's a
step that we aren't built to take, Jim ... do
you understand me?"

"I think so, Oran," answered Jim.

"... But at other times," went on the
Emperor. Jim could not tell whether Oran
had noted his answer or not. "... But at
other times, things only start to get sharp
and clear—and when I try to look more
closely, they go very fuzzy, and out of focus,
and large. And I lose that sense of extra,
inner sharp sight that I had to begin with.
Then I have bad dreams for a while—
dreams, awake and asleep. It's in dreams
like that, that I've seen the Blue Beast, three
times now. . . ."

The Emperor's voice trailed off again, and
Jim thought that they had come merely to
another temporary pause in the conversa-

tion. But abruptly the Emperor's hand fell from his shoulder.

Jim stopped and turned. He found Oran looking down at him, smiling, clear-eyed and cheerful.

"Well, I mustn't keep you, Jim," said Oran in a thoroughly normal, conversational voice. "This will be your first party—and after all, you're practically the guest of honor. Why don't you circulate and meet people. I've got to go find Vhotan. He worries too much when I'm away from him."

The Emperor vanished. Jim stood still, and the cleared circle of floor began to fill in around him, as those on the outskirts drifted inward, and new arrivals began to appear. He looked about for Ro but could not see her.

"Adok!" he said in a low voice.

The Starkien appeared beside him.

"Forgive me, Jim," said Adok. "I didn't know that the Emperor was through talking to you. I found the servant you sent me to find."

"Take me where I can see him but he can't see me," said Jim.

Abruptly they were in a narrow, shadowy place between two pillars, looking toward a further area where a cluster of close pillars enclosed a small open space, where a large number of trays loaded with food and drink stood neatly racked in the empty air, one above another. Standing amidst these trays was a servant, one of the short brown men with the long hair. Jim and Adok stood behind him, and looking past him, they could see out to where another servant was circulating within view with a tray of food.

"Good," said Jim.

He memorized the location and shifted both himself and Adok back to where he had been standing when the Emperor had left him.

"Adok," he said softly, "I'm going to try to stay continuously within sight of the Emperor. I'd like you to stay within sight of me, but not exactly with me. Keep your eyes on me, and when I disappear, I want you to go to Vhotan, who'll be with the Emperor, and tell him I want him to be a witness to something. Then bring him to the place where that servant is. You understand?"

"Yes, Jim," said Adok unemotionally.

"Now," said Jim. "How do I find the Emperor?"

"I can take you to him," said Adok. "All Starkiens can always find the Emperor, at any time. It's in case one of us should be needed."

They were suddenly elsewhere in the Great Gathering Room. Jim looked about and from a distance of a couple of dozen feet saw the Emperor—this time without a circle of privacy around him, talking and laughing with several other High-born. Vhotan, his yellowish brows knitted, was at the younger man's elbow.

Jim looked around him again and discovered Adok looking at him from perhaps twenty feet away. Jim nodded and drifted off at an angle that would keep him moving through the crowd, but at about always the same distance from the Emperor.

Twice the Emperor shifted position suddenly. Twice Jim found himself shifted by Adok to a new position within sight of the High-born ruler. Surprisingly, through all this, none of the High-born around Jim paid particular attention to him. They seemed to have no eagerness to see the Wolfling in whose honor the party was being given, and if their eyes rested on him unknowingly, they evidently took him for simply one more of the servants.

Time stretched out. Nearly an hour had gone by, and Jim was almost beginning to doubt his earlier certainties, when abruptly he saw what he had been waiting for.

At first glance, it was nothing much. The Emperor was half-turned away from Jim, and all that betrayed his change in condition was a slight stiffening of his tall figure. He had become somewhat immobile, somewhat rigid.

Jim hastily took two steps to the left so that he could catch sight of the man's face. Oran was staring through and past the other High-born man he had been talking to. His gaze was fixed; his smile was fixed; and as at the bullfight, there was a little trickle of moisture shining at the corner of his mouth.

None of those around him appeared to be in the least aware of this. But Jim wasted no time watching them. Instead, he turned to look about for servants. He had made less than a half-turn before he saw the first man, a thin black-haired member of the lesser races, carrying a silver tray of what looked like small cakes.

The man was not moving. He was stopped, still, as frozen in position as the Emperor.

Jim hastily completed his turn. He saw three more servants, all of them rigid, all of them unmoving as statues. Even as he looked, the High-born around them began to take notice of this strange lack of activity in their midst. But Jim did not wait to see how their reaction would develop. Instantly he transferred himself to the shadowy area behind the servant with the trays—to that place where Adok had earlier taken him.

The man with the trays was standing, looking. But he was not rigid—as was the servant who could be seen a couple of dozen yards beyond him, surrounded by High-born.

Jim bent nearly double and ran forward swiftly and silently behind the trays until he came up with the servant who was looking out. At once he caught the man from behind with both hands. One hand taking him at the top and back of the neck just under the overhang of the skull, the other hand caught hold of the left armpit from behind, with the thumb resting over a pressure point just to the left of the shoulder-blade.

"Move," whispered Jim swiftly, "and I'll break your neck."

The man stiffened. But he made no sound, and he did not move.

"Now," whispered Jim again. "Do exactly as I tell you—"

He paused to glance around behind him. There, in the shadows, he saw the stocky form of Adok, and with Adok a towering High-born shape that would be Vhotan. Jim turned back to the servant.

"Put the two first fingers of your right hand across the biceps of your left arm," Jim whispered to the man.

The other did not move. Still keeping himself crouched low and hidden behind the servant's form, Jim pushed his thumb in again against the pressure point.

For a long moment the man resisted. Then, jerkily, almost like a robot, he moved his right hand up, up, and laid the forefingers of it, extended in V form, across the biceps of his left arm.

Outside, the immobile servant in sight suddenly began to move, as if nothing had happened, trailed by a small cloud of puzzled and interested High-born. Jim quickly clapped a hand over the mouth of the man he was holding, and half-lifted, half-dragged him back into the shadows.

Vhotan and Adok came forward to face down at the man.

"Now—" began Vhotan grimly. But at that moment the servant made an odd, small noise and suddenly slumped, heavy in Jim's grasp.

"Yes," said Vhotan, as if Jim's laying the man down had been a comment in words, "whoever planned this wouldn't have taken any chances on leaving him alive for us to question. Even the brain structure will be destroyed, no doubt."

He raised his eyes and looked across the dead body to Jim. His High-born mind had plainly already deduced much of what Jim had brought him here to see. But Vhotan's eyes retained a bit of their chill, nonetheless.

"Do you know who's behind all this?" he asked Jim.

Jim shook his head.

"But you clearly expected it to happen," said Vhotan. "You expected it enough to send your Starkien to bring me here.—Why me?"

Jim looked unstaringly at him.

"Because I decided you were the one man among the High-born who had to admit to yourself, consciously, that the Emperor's mind is not all it should be—or perhaps," said Jim, for a second remembering their talk, his and the Emperor's, as they walked up and down the polished floor, "his mind is a little too much more than it should be."

A faint click seemed to come from the throat of Vhotan. It was several long seconds before he said anything; and when he did speak, it was on another topic.

"How did you find out about this—this, that the servants had planned?" Vhotan asked.

"I didn't find out, to the point where I was absolutely sure it would happen," said Jim. "But I taught myself the Silent Language of the servants underground and learned that something was in the wind. Putting that together with this party, and the Emperor's known frailty, gave me an idea of what to look for. So when I got here, I sent Adok around to look for it; and when he found it, I acted as you've just seen."

Vhotan had stiffened again at the coupling of the words "Emperor" and "frailty." But he relaxed as Jim finished talking, and nodded.

"You've done a good job, Wolfling," he said; and the words were plain enough, even though the tone was grudging. "From this point on, I'll handle it. But we'd better get you off the Throne World for a while, sponsored for adoption or not sponsored for adoption."

He stood and thought for a second.

"I think the Emperor will promote you," he said finally. "As a rank more commensurate with your effective High-born status as someone sponsored for adoption, he'll promote you to a Starkien Commander of Ten-units and send you off on some military-police job on one of the Colony Worlds."

He turned away from Jim, Adok, and the dead servant, as if about to disappear. Then, apparently changing his mind, he swung back to look at Jim again.

"What's your name?" he said sharply.

"Jim," answered Jim.

"Jim. Well, you did a good job, Jim," said Vhotan grimly. "The Emperor appreciates it. And—so do I."

With that, he did disappear.

Chapter 8

The planet Athiya to which Jim was sent with his Ten-units of Starkien, Adok, and Harn II—who was the Ten-units' original commander but now acting-adjutant to Jim—was one of the many worlds populated by the small brown men with long, straight hair hanging down their back. The Governor, a burly little chestnut of a man, avoided all references to the uprising, to put down which he had asked the High-born to send him Starkien help. He insisted that they go through a large and formal welcoming ceremony, during which he avoided all references to the uprising and any questions about it made to him by Jim.

However, explanations could not be put off forever. Jim, Harn II, Adok, and the Governor all ended up at last in the Governor's private office of the capital city of Athiya. The Governor attempted to fuss around getting them hassocks and refreshments, but Jim cut him short.

"Never mind that," said Jim. "We don't want food and drink. We want to know about this uprising—where is it, how many people are involved, and what kind of weapons have they?"

The Governor sat down on one of the Hassocks and abruptly burst into tears.

For a moment Jim was dumbfounded. Then knowledge that had its roots not in what he had learned on the Throne World as much as what he had learned back in his anthropological studies on Earth reassured him with the obvious deduction that the Governor belonged to a culture in which it was not unusual for the males to cry—even as publicly and noisily as the Governor was doing now.

Jim waited, therefore, until the Governor had gotten rid of his first explosion of emotion, and then put his question again.

Snuffling, the Governor wiped tears from his eyes and tried to answer. "I never thought they wouldn't send me a High-born in command of the Starkiens!" he said thickly to Jim. "I was going to throw myself on his mercy . . . but you're not a High-born—"

His tears threatened to flood his explanations once again. Jim spoke sharply to him, to bring him out of it.

"Stand up!" Jim snapped. Reflexively, the Governor obeyed. "As a matter of fact, I've been sponsored for adoption into the High-born. But that's beside the point. Whatever the Emperor sent you is what your situation deserves."

"But it isn't!" choked the Governor. "I—I lied. It isn't just an uprising. It's a revolution! All the other families on the planet have joined together—even my cousin Cluth is with them. In fact, he's the head of it all. They've all banded together to kill me and put Cluth here in my place!"

"What's this?" demanded Jim. He was aware that the Colony Worlds of the empire had their miniature courts, modeled on the Throne World's. These courts consisted of the noble families of the Colony World, headed up by the family and person of the Governor, who was a small Emperor locally, in his own right.

"Why did you let it get this far?" put in Harn II. "Why didn't you use your colonial troops earlier to put it down?"

"I—I—" The Governor wrung his hands, obviously incapable of speech.

Watching him, Jim had no doubt what had happened. His studies of the past few weeks, both underground and at the learning-center screen in Ro's apartment, once he had trained himself to read at the rapid High-born rate, had given him a good insight not merely into Throne World society but into the society of these Colony Worlds. Undoubtedly the Governor had let things get this far out of hand because he had been confident of his own ability until recently to bargain with the dissident elements of his world. Evidently he had underrated his opposition.

Then, having let things get out of hand,
he had been afraid to admit the fact to the
Throne World and had put in a request for
much less in the way of Starkien troops
than he needed to control the situation, possibly imagining he could use the Starkiens
coming as a threat and still make a deal
with the rebels.

However, understanding this was no help
now. The Throne World was committed to
backing up the Governors, who were allowed to hold power on the Colony Worlds.

"Sir," said Harn II, tapping Jim on the
elbow. He beckoned to Jim, and they walked
aside, where they could talk privately at
the far end of the room. Adok followed them,
leaving the Governor standing, a lonely little brown figure surrounded by hassocks
and floating table surfaces.

"Sir," said Harn II in a low voice, once
they had stopped at the far end of the room,
"I strongly suggest that we stay put here
and send a message back to the Throne
World for additional Starkiens. If half what
that man there says is true, those who are
against him will already have control of
most of the colonial armed forces. A Ten-
units of Starkiens can do a lot, but they
can't be expected to defeat armies. There's
no reason we should lose men just because
of *his* blunder."

"No," said Jim. "Of course not. On the
other hand, I think I'd like to look into the
situation a little further and see for our-

selves what we're up against before shouting for help. So far the only account of things is what we've gotten from the Governor. Things may be a great deal different from what he thinks, even if everything he's afraid of is true."

"Sir," said Harn II, "I have to protest. Every Starkien is an expensive and valuable man in terms of his training and equipment. They shouldn't be risked in a hopeless cause; and as their former commander, I have to tell you I think it isn't fair to them to risk them that way."

"Sir," said Adok—since they had left the Throne World, Adok also had been addressing him with military respectfulness—"the Adjutant-Commander is right."

Jim looked at both of the Starkiens in turn. They were subtly reminding him of the fact that while Jim was in nominal command of the expedition, the only one with real experience as a commander of Starkien Ten-units in that room was Harn himself.

"I appreciate your objections, Adjutant," said Jim slowly to Harn II now. "But I'd still like to look the situation over."

"Yes, sir," said Harn II. There was not the slightest flicker of emotion visible in him at being overruled. How much of this was normal Starkien self-control, and how much of it was Harn's own resignation to the situation, was something Jim could not tell. But Jim turned now and led the way back across the room to the Governor, who looked up hopelessly as they came to him.

"There are a good many things I want to know," said Jim. "But you can start out by telling me what it was your cousin—or whoever it was who's behind this insurrection—used in order to get the others to join him."

The Governor started to wring his hands and cloud up toward tears again, but on meeting Jim's eye, evidently thought better of it.

"I don't know . . . I don't know!" he said. "There was some talk about their having protection. Protection . . ." He trailed off timorously.

"Go on," said Jim. "Finish what you were going to say."

"Protection . . . from someone on the Throne World," said the Governor fearfully.

"Protection by one of the High-born?" demanded Jim bluntly.

"I—I never exactly heard them say so, now!" chattered the Governor, paling. "I didn't ever really hear that said in so many words!"

"Don't worry about it," said Jim. "Now, listen to me. Your cousin and his allies undoubtedly have armed forces. Where are they, and how many of them are there?"

With the topic off the High-born and back on his own people, the Governor revived like a wilted flower. His burly little shoulders twitched, and his voice deepened, as he turned and pointed off through the walls of his office.

"North of here." He gave a distance in Imperial units that amounted to something under sixty miles. "They're camped on a plain with a ring of hills around it. They've got sentry posts up on the hill, and the posts are manned by the best men in our colonial armed forces."

"How many of those are with them?"

"Three—three—" the Governor stuttered with new apprehension, "—three-quarters, maybe."

"More likely ninety-eight percent of them, sir," put in Harn II, gazing at the Governor, "if he estimates them as high as three-quarters."

"Why haven't they moved into your capital city here before now?" asked Jim.

"I . . . I told them you were coming," said the Governor miserably. "In fact I . . . offered to send you away if they'd make terms."

"The only terms to be made," said Harn II to the little man, "will be by us. How many men does ninety-eight percent of your colonial armed forces amount to?"

"Three divisions," stammered the Governor, "about forty thousand trained and armed men."

"Sixty to seventy thousand," amended Harn II, looking at Jim.

Jim nodded.

"Very well," he said. He looked out a

long, low window in one side of the office. "It's almost sunset locally. Do you have a moon?" he added, turning to the Governor.

"Two of them—" the Governor was beginning, when Jim cut him short.

"One would be enough, if it gives us enough moonlight," he said. He turned to Harn and Adok. "As soon as it's dark, we'll go up and have a look at that camp of theirs."

He looked back at the Governor, who bobbed his head, smiling.

"And we'll take you with us," said Jim.

The Governor's smile vanished as suddenly as the smile of a cartoon figure wiped from the drawing by the cartoonist's eraser. Four hours later, with the earlier of the two moons just beginning to show a small orange rim over the low hills of the horizon surrounding the capital city, Jim, with Harn and Adok up front and the Governor in the rear of a small, completely enclosed combat reconnaissance craft, lifted out of the capital city, rose into the darkness of the night sky just below the black belly of some overhanging clouds, and slid silently northward in the direction the Governor indicated. Some fifteen minutes later they descended close to the ground and approached the hills ringing the plain they sought, with the underside of the reconnaissance vessel brushing the heads of the three-foot-tall grass as it dodged in and out of clumps of elmlike trees.

When the terrain began to tilt upward toward the encircling hills themselves, they hid the reconnaissance vessel in a clump of brush and young trees and continued the rest of the way on foot. The two Starkiens, together, went first, spread out about fifteen yards apart. They moved with an amazing silence, which Jim was able to match only because of his hunting experience back on Earth. But most surprising of them all was the little Governor, who turned out to be quite at home stealing quietly through the patches of alternate moonlight and shadow. Once he was sure the small man could keep up and would make no noise, Jim spread out from him to approximately the same distance existing between Adok and Harn.

They were nearly to the top of the slope that would at last allow them to overlook the plain beyond when the two Starkiens dropped suddenly out of sight on their stomachs in the grass. Jim and the Governor immediately did the same.

Some minutes went by. Then Adok suddenly rose from the grass immediately before Jim.

"It's all right, sir. Come on. You can walk the rest of the way," he said. "The sentry was asleep."

Jim and the Governor got to their feet and followed the Starkien up the slope and into a little enclosure perhaps a dozen feet across, fenced in with what looked like a silver-wire mesh perhaps a yard high. In the center of the enclosure was an instrument resembling a beach umbrella with the fabric removed from the ribs supporting it. The sentry Adok had mentioned was nowhere in sight.

"There's the camp," said Harn, pointing over the far rim of the wire mesh and down a further slope. "It's all right. You can speak up inside the fence, sir. We can't be seen or heard now."

Jim walked over to stand beside Harn and look down. What he saw looked not so much like an armed camp as a circular small town or city of dome-shaped buildings divided by streets into pie-shaped sections.

"Come here," he said, looking back at the Governor. The Governor came obediently up to the wire mesh. "Look down there. Tell me. Do you see anything unusual about that camp down there?"

The Governor gazed and finally shook his head.

"Sir," said Harn, "the camp is laid out according to one of the customary military patterns, with different groups or units in each section, and a guard of men from each section to complete the perimeter circuit."

"Except they've set up a council building!" said the Governor self-pityingly. "Look at that! Just as if I was there with them!"

"Where?" asked Jim.

The Governor pointed out a larger dome-shaped building just to the right of the geometric center of the camp.

"Only a Governor is supposed to call a council among the troops!" he said. "But they've been going ahead, anyway. As if I were deposed already—or even dead!" He snuffled.

"What are you suspicious of, sir?" asked Harn. Adok had moved up close behind them. Jim could now see him out of the corner of his eye.

"I'm not exactly sure," said Jim. "Adjutant, what kind of weapons do our Starkiens have that these colonial soldiers wouldn't have?"

"We have vastly better individual defensive screens," answered Harn. "Also, each of our men represents fire power equal to that of one of their heavy companies."

"Then it's just a case of having the same sort of weapons, only better ones?" said Jim. "Is that it?"

"Sir," answered Harn, "the greatest weapon of the Starkiens is the trained individual Starkien himself. He—"

"Yes, I know that," interrupted Jim a little sharply. "What about"—he fumbled in his mind for means of translating the Earth terms there into the Empire language— "what about large fixed weapons? Unusually powerful explosives—nuclear fusion or fission weapons?"

"These colonials aren't allowed the technological machinery to make large fixed weapons," said Harn. "It's possible that they might secretly have built some sort of fission device—but unlikely. As for any antimatter weapon, that's completely impossible—"

"Just a minute," Jim interrupted him. "Do the Starkiens have all these things available back on the Throne World? The—what was it you called it? Antimatter devices?"

"Of course. But they haven't been required for use off the Throne World for some thousands of years," said Harn. "Are you aware of what an antimatter device is, sir?"

"Only," said Jim grimly, "to the extent of knowing that a little bit of antimatter coming in contact with a little bit of matter can cause a good deal of destruction."

He stood for a second without saying anything. Then he spoke abruptly.

"Well, Adjutant," he said to Harn, "now that you've seen how things look down there, do you still want to send back to the Throne World for help?"

"No, sir," answered Harn promptly. "If the sentry we surprised in his post is at all representative, their armed forces are incredibly poor. Also, their camp seems set up more for the convenience of those dwelling in it than with any eye to overall defense. The pattern is there, but there are no street patrols, no perimeter patrols that I can see, and—most amazing—no overhead warning system whatsoever. Those people down there are just going through the motions of being an army."

Harn stopped, as if giving Jim a chance to comment.

"Go on, Adjutant," said Jim.

"Sir," acknowledged Harn, "what with what I've mentioned, the fact that we've just now discovered that their leaders are all concentrated in that one building, makes the military solution to this situation extremely simple. I'd suggest we send Adok back for the rest of the men right now, and as soon as they get here we mount a raid on that one building, coming down on it from directly overhead so as to avoid triggering their perimeter defenses, and either kill or capture the ringleaders. Then they can be returned to the capital city for trial."

"And what," asked Jim, "if the rumor the Governor heard was correct—that these rebels have a friend among the High-born on the Throne World?"

"Sir?" said Harn. Insofar as a Starkien could, he sounded puzzled. "It's impossible, of course, for a High-born to have any dealings with colonial revolutionists like those down there. But even assuming that they down there had such a friend, there's nothing he could do to stop us. And, moreover, we Starkiens are responsible only to the Emperor."

"Yes," said Jim. "All the same, Adjutant, I'm not going to follow your advice here, any more than I followed it when you suggested earlier that we send back to the Throne World for reinforcements."

He turned away from Harn to confront the little Governor.

"Your noble families are always fighting with each other, aren't they?" he asked.

"Why—they're nearly always intriguing against me, all of them!" said the little Governor. Then he giggled unexpectedly. "Oh, I see what you mean, Commander. Yes, they do fight among one another a lot. In fact, if they didn't, I might have some trouble handling them. Oh, yes, their main sport is intriguing and accusing one another of everything you can think of."

"Naturally," said Jim, half to himself. "They're *noyaux*."

"Sir?" said Harn beside him. The little Governor was also looking puzzled. The scientific term in the language of Earth meant nothing to them.

"Never mind," said Jim. He went on to the Governor, "Would there be anyone among these other leaders down there that your cousin generally doesn't get along with?"

"Someone who Cluth doesn't—" The little Governor stopped thoughtfully. He stood a second, gazing at the moonlit grass at his feet. "Notral! Yes, if there's anyone he isn't likely to get along with, it would be Notral."

He turned and pointed down at the encampment.

"See?" he said. "Cluth's people will be in that slice there of the encampment. And Notral's will be way over there, almost directly opposite. The farther they are away from each other usually, the better they like it!"

"Adjutant. Adok," said Jim, turning to the two Starkiens. "I've got a special job for you. Do you suppose that you could go down there quietly and bring back to me, alive and in good shape, a perimeter guard from the section just outside Notral's area of the encampment?"

"Of course, sir," answered Harn.

"Fine," said Jim. "Be sure to blindfold him when you take him from the perimeter. And you'll have to blindfold him again when you take him back. Now"—he turned to the Governor—"point them out Notral's area of the encampment again."

The Governor did so. The two Starkiens let themselves out of the sentry post and effectually disappeared—as effectually as if they had translated themselves from there to some other spot, in the fashion of the Throne World. It was a little over half an hour, by earthly standards, before they returned, and Jim saw the section of the mesh fence of the sentry post swing open. He had been sitting on the ground, cross-legged, with the little Governor sitting to one side of him. But now Jim got to his feet, and the Governor scrambled up, as ordered, to stand alongside him, his extreme short-ness emphasizing Jim's six-foot-four.

Adok crawled into the sentry post and stood up, to be followed a second later by a small brown youngster in a straplike harness somewhat like that of the Starkiens. The young colonial soldier was so frightened that he shook visibly. Harn followed closely behind him and shut the mesh gate once he was inside.

"Bring him here," said Jim, imitating the breathy, hissing accents of the Throne World High-born. He was standing so that his back was to the rising moon, which had finally been joined by its smaller partner of the skies. Their combined light flooded over his shoulder and showed him clearly the face of the small long-haired soldier but left his own face in the darkness of deep shadow.

"Do you know who it is I have chosen to be your final leader?" Jim asked in a hard, deep-voiced tone when the young soldier was almost literally carried by the two Starkiens to stand before him.

The colonial soldier's teeth chattered so badly he could not make a coherent answer. But he shook his head violently. Jim made a short sound of anger and contempt, deep in his throat.

"Never mind," he said harshly. "You know who controls the area behind your section of the perimeter?"

"Yes. . . ." The young soldier nodded his head eagerly.

"Go to him," said Jim. "Tell him I've changed my plans. He's to take over command of your people now, without waiting."

Jim waited. The young soldier trembled.

"Do you understand me?" Jim shot at him.

The prisoner went into a violent convulsion of nodding.

"Good," said Jim. "Adok, take him outside. I want a word with my adjutant before you go."

Adok shepherded the prisoner out beyond the mesh fence. Jim turned and beckoned both Harn and the Governor to him. He pointed down at the camp.

"Now," he said to the Governor, "point out to the adjutant the part of the perimeter lying outside the area that your cousin Cluth will be occupying."

The Governor shrank a little from Jim, apparently infected by the fear of the prisoner, and stretched out a trembling forefinger to indicate to Harn the section Jim had mentioned. Harn asked a few questions to make certain of the location and then turned to Jim.

"You want me to take the prisoner back there?" he asked Jim.

"That's right, Adjutant," said Jim.

"Yes, sir," said Harn, and went out through the mesh fence.

This time the trip took them nearer an hour of earthly time. The moment they returned, with word that they had set the prisoner to walking forward and heard him challenged and picked up by the soldiers of Cluth's perimeter, Jim ordered them all out of the sentry post and back down the slope toward their vessel.

They went swiftly, at Jim's orders. It was not until they were fully airborne that Jim relaxed. Then he ordered Adok, who was at the controls, to take the ship up and out to the farthest possible distance from which their night-vision screens could keep view on the camp. Adok obeyed. Some six or eight minutes later they settled into a circling patrol some fifteen thousand feet up and ten miles' ground distance from the camp. As silently as a cloud itself, the reconnaissance vessel swung like a huge toy at the end of an invisible string better than ten miles long about the drowsy armed camp below.

Jim sat unmoving, gazing at the night-vision screen in the control area beyond Adok, up in the front of the ship. With him sat Harn, the Governor, and, for that matter, Adok himself, all gazing at the screen, but, with the exception of Jim, with no idea of what they were watching for.

For quite a while it seemed that their watch would produce nothing out of the ordinary. Reaching out, Jim worked the telescopic controls of the night screen, from time to time zooming in for a view of the streets and buildings. The night patrols were going their rounds without incident. Most of the buildings were dark. And so it continued.

Then, without warning, there was a little

wink of light, hardly brighter than the blink of a flashlight, in what seemed the center of the Governor's council-quarters building.

"I think that's—" Jim was beginning, when Harn threw himself past him, literally tore the control out of Adok's hands, and sent the small craft twisting away, fleeing at top speed from the scene they had just been watching.

Adok, trained soldier that he was, did not fight his superior officer except for a first instinctive grab at the controls as they were taken from him. He slipped out of the control seat and let Harn take his place.

Jim leaned forward and spoke in Harn's ear.

"Antimatter?" Jim asked.

Harn nodded. A moment later the shock wave hit, and the little vessel went tumbling end over end through the night sky, like some insignificant insect swatted by the paw of some monster.

Harn, clinging to the controls, finally got the ship back on an even keel. Within, they were all of them battered to a certain extent. The little Governor was only half-conscious, and his nose was bleeding. Jim helped Adok to prop the little man up on his feet and buckle his seat harness around him. Ironically, not one of them had his harness buckled at the moment they had been struck by the shock wave.

"Is there any point in our going back?" Jim asked Harn. The adjutant shook his head. "There'll be nothing to see," he said. "Only a crater."

"How much antimatter would you judge was involved in that?" Jim asked.

Harn shook his head.

"I'm no expert in amounts, sir," he said. "The total *unit* is about as big as you can hold comfortably in one hand. But that's for convenience. The effective element inside it may be no larger than a grain of sand, for all I know. . . . Sir?"

"Yes?" said Jim.

"If I may ask, sir," said Harn evenly, "what made you believe that there was antimatter down in that camp?"

"It was a guess, Adjutant," said Jim somberly. "Based on a lot of factors—here and back on the Throne World."

"It was a trap, then," said Harn, without perceptible emotion in his voice. "A trap for me and my—I beg your pardon, sir—your Starkiens. We were meant to go in through the door they left open—that unguarded direct descent upon the main building. The whole Ten-unit would have been wiped out."

He was silent.

"But, sir," said Adok, looking first at him, then turning to Jim, "these colonials must've known that they'd be wiped out too?"

"What makes you think they'd know, Starkien?" said Harn. "There was no reason that whoever supplied them with that antimatter should have wanted them to know what they were handling."

Adok subsided. After a few moments Harn spoke again to Jim.

"Sir?" he said. "Could I ask the commander what *noyaux* are?"

"Social groups, Adjutant," said Jim. "Family groups whose chief occupation is badgering, insulting, and struggling with other family groups in every way short of actual fighting."

"These"—Harn glanced for a moment at the Governor—"form *noyaux?*"

"Their chief families do," said Jim. "Ordinarily their bickering just gives them something to do, because subconsciously they don't intend to harm each other, no matter how much they may believe consciously that they're ready to fight at the drop of a hat. But the point is, the *noyaux* never trust each other. When that soldier of Notral's perimeter guard was brought in and questioned, Cluth leaped at the conclusion that he had been betrayed by whomever from the Throne World gave him the antimatter. He made an effort to take it back from wherever it was being guarded, and some accident set it off. I hadn't hoped for that so much as for a splitting up of the encampment, which would give us a chance to swoop down on Cluth's party and take the antimatter back from him."

"I see, sir," said Harn. He said nothing for a second. "And now, sir?"

"Now," said Jim grimly, "we head back to the Throne World as quickly as possible."

"Sir!" acknowledged Harn.

He said no more after that, and both Jim and Adok sat without speaking. In the little vessel there was silence, until the Governor, recovering full consciousness, began to mourn his dead cousin, with mutterings of Cluth's name, and stifled, low-voiced sobs.

Chapter 9

The ship that had brought Jim and the Starkiens to this world was a smaller version of the space-going vessel that had brought Jim back from Alpha Centauri III. It was just big enough to hold the Ten-units of men, and required only one individual on duty watch in the ship's Power Room. It was directed by the same economical method according to which most things owned by the High-born were run. Whoever was in command of the ship merely visualized his destination and left it to the ship to pick up that visualization, resolve it, match it with the destination itself, and bring the ship to it. On their outward-bound voyage from the Throne World, it had been Harn II who had directed the ship, since Jim had no mental picture of their destination. Now, headed back to the Throne World, Jim needed no help. He needed only to visualize any spot on the surface of the Throne World— his own quarters, if need be—and the ship would take over from there. He did so, and the ship obeyed.

As they were about to land, however, he took Harn II and Adok aside.

"Adjutant," he said to Harn, "I want you to keep the men aboard ship here after we land. Don't go directly to your quarters to report back. Wait here in the ship until I send for you."

Harn stood still without saying anything for a long second.

"This is against usual practice," he said at last. "I assume it's an order?"

"It's an order," said Jim.

"In that case ..." said Harn, "the only thing that can override it would be either orders from the Emperor or reason for us to believe that our staying aboard would be contrary to the Emperor's wishes. After what we've been through, I'm inclined not to think that these orders of yours can be contrary to the Emperor's wishes."

"You can believe me, Adjutant," said Jim slowly. "It's the Emperor's welfare I'm concerned about. And that welfare may be better served if you men stay out of sight aboard this ship instead of going back to your quarters."

"Sir!" said Harn II acknowledgingly. "You're returning to your own quarters, Sir?"

"I am," said Jim, "and I'm taking Adok with me."

He touched Adok on the arm and shifted them both back into his own quarters. They were empty. He shifted to Ro's apartment.

Ro was there, in the room with all her pets—hers and Afuan's—cutting the nails of the apelike creature. But she dropped her tools and practically tackled him in her enthusiasm at seeing him again.

"Jim!" she said. "*Jim!* . . ."

He let her squeeze him for a moment, and hugged her back briefly. Then, patting her head gently, he reached behind him and unlocked the grip of her hands so as to put her arms away from him.

"I'm sorry," he said gently. "But the situation's rather urgent."

She giggled, almost wickedly, ignoring the fact that he held her hands. Her eyes ran over him.

"Is that your Starkien uniform?" she asked. "How big you look in it! . . . Are those bands you're wearing still powered?"

"Yes," said Jim, not knowing quite what to make of this sudden, mad humor of hers, and hoping that a calm answer would calm her as well.

"They are?" she giggled again. "Show me! Smash that wall there down for me—"

She broke off suddenly and did sober up.

"No, no. What am I saying?" Abruptly the ridiculous humor was gone from her. She looked up at him gravely. "What is it Jim? You look worried!"

"Worried?" He let go of her wrists. "Not exactly—but there may be something going on to be worried about. Tell me, Ro. What on the Throne World here is blue?"

"Blue? You mean the color blue?" she asked. He nodded his head. "Why . . . white is the color we usually use. You know that. Occasionally, a little red. I don't think there is much blue on the Throne World nowadays, except a stray object or two that one of the High-born might've brought back from one of the Colonial Worlds."

"Think," said Jim, staring steadily at her. "Think hard."

"But, there really isn't any—oh," Ro interrupted herself, "unless you want to count the usual things. The sky here is blue. And the water is blue. Oh, and"—she paused to smile again—"there's the Emperor's Blue Beast still hidden somewhere in the palace someplace, if you want to count that."

"Blue Beast?" His question was so sharp and abrupt that she paled.

"Why, yes, Jim," she said, staring at him, "but it's nothing. It's just a toy that he used to have when he was a baby. Only he started to have nightmares about it, and they hid it from him. I don't know who hid it, or where it was hidden, and I don't think anybody knows nowadays. But it got so bad that anything blue-colored was likely to—upset him. That's why there's never anything blue left lying around where the Emperor might see it. Why is it so important to you?"

He heard the question at the end of her speech, but it was like hearing an unimportant noise far off. His mind was whirring, and he did not bother to answer her.

"I've got to see Vhotan right away," he said. "How do I find him, Ro?"

"Jim, what is it?" She was really alarmed now. "Vhotan's with the Emperor. You can't just go charging in on the Emperor. Oh, I know you did it once and got away with it. But you can't do it now. Particularly now."

"Why, particularly now?" Jim asked.

She took a small step back from him.

"Jim . . ." she said, uncertainly. "Don't . . ."

Jim made an effort to return his face to calmness.

"All right," he said. "Now tell me. Why is now so particular?"

"It's just that right now there's all this trouble going on, on the Colony Worlds," said Ro. "Vhotan's been sending out Starkiens to help the Governors of the lesser races put down the trouble, until there aren't any left here on the Throne World. He doesn't have a moment to spare to talk to anyone—"

She broke off, staring at him again. *"Jim, will you tell me what it is!"*

But again he hardly heard her. His thoughts were galloping far ahead under the impetus of this new piece of information. For a moment he gazed unseeingly out the transparent window of the pets' room at the ocean shore.—An ocean shore, here too? The idea that Ro must carry a sandy beach and a piece of ocean around with her to provide a view for Afuan's pets was so ridiculous that it jolted his thoughts back into effectiveness.

"I want to get in touch with Slothiel," he said, looking back at Ro. "Then, the four of us—you, I, Slothiel, and Adok—must go and find Vhotan, whether he's with the Emperor or not."

"Are you crazy, Jim?" she said. "You can't go into the Emperor's presence wearing power bands like that! No one's allowed in his presence with anything more than a rod. His Starkiens would kill you out of reflex the minute you appeared. If you have to do this wild thing, at least take those power bands off!—You too, Adok!"

She glanced past him at the Starkien. Her own fingers were already busy stripping the power bands off Jim's left arm. The wisdom of what she said was undeniable, and after a second he began to assist her. A moment later he had no weapon left but the rod in its loops at his belt. Looking around, he saw that Adok had similarly rid himself of power bands.

"Now," he said to Ro. "To Slothiel's. You'll have to find him for us. I don't even know where his quarters are."

She touched his arm, and they were abruptly in a different suite of rooms.

"Slothiel!" called Jim. But no answer came back through any of the three doorways leading off from the room in which they had appeared.

"He's not here," said Ro. "And it's no use

our moving all over the Throne World looking for him. He could be one jump ahead of us, and we'd never catch up with him that way. The best thing is just to wait here for him, Jim."

"Wait?" said Jim. "Waiting is the one thing we can't afford to do. Can't we—"

He broke off. For Slothiel had just appeared before them.

"Welcome home, Jim," said Slothiel. "You're the first of our conquering heroes to get back. I heard you'd landed ship, but when I went to your quarters just now, you weren't there. I tried Ro's—and all I found was a batch of discarded power bands. So I came back here to look for messages—and, here you are!"

He smiled and waved Ro and Jim graciously to hassocks. Adok he ignored.

"Sit down," Slothiel said. "How about something to eat and drink? I can get you—"

"Nothing!" interrupted Jim. "Slothiel, are you loyal to the Emperor?"

Slothiel raised his eyebrows.

"My dear ex-Wolfling," he drawled, "*all* High-born are loyal to the Emperor.—Otherwise how could we be loyal to ourselves?"

"There's loyalty and loyalty," said Jim bluntly. "I didn't ask you if you were loyal, in the academic sense. I asked you if you were loyal in the—say—Starkien sense?"

Slothiel stiffened slightly. His white eyebrows drew together.

"What sort of catechism is this, Jim?" he

asked. But the tone of his voice was no longer one of completely idle banter. Under a surface of indifference there was a note of hard interest.

"You haven't answered me, Slothiel," said Jim.

"Should I answer, then?" murmured Slothiel in the tone of voice of a man choosing between two canapés on a serving tray. But his eyes remained unmoving on Jim. "After all, I am a High-born, and this is only an ex-Wolfling, a being of the lesser races ... yes, I will answer. I'm loyal, Jim." His voice had suddenly become hard, with none of the soft nonsense left about it. "Now, what is this? And I want a straight, direct answer!"

"My Ten-units of Starkiens on Athiya," said Jim evenly, "were baited into a military trap that would have been no trap at all, if it hadn't been equipped with an anti-matter weapon."

"Antimatter?" Slothiel's face stiffened for a second in astonishment, then quickly relaxed again as his High-born mind accepted the incredible statement and ran quickly on to examine the implications of it. Within a few seconds he looked at Jim again. "Yes, you're right, Jim. We should see Vhotan about this."

"That's what I've intended to do, all along," said Jim. "I was only waiting to find you and take you along with the rest of us."

"Rest of us?" Slothiel glanced at Ro and Adok. "You and I are sufficient."

"No," said Jim. "I need Adok with me as a witness to what happened. And Ro stays with us because it's safest for her."

"Safest?" Slothiel shot a glance at Ro, who was watching both men and looking puzzled. "Oh—yes, I see what you mean. She could be taken and used as a hostage against you by whoever's behind this if we left her unprotected. All right, Starkien!"

He beckoned Adok in close, and the four of them shifted as a group to their destination.

They appeared in a room that was not the same room in which Jim had encountered Vhotan and the Emperor before. This was a larger room, something like a ballroom with a lounge area at one end. All the other walls of the ballroom except that which opened upon the lounge area were covered to the high, white ceiling with light-green draperies. In the center of the ballroom floor sat a peculiar instrument with a basketball-shaped head that was slowly rotating. In time with its rotation, various patterns in many colors other than blue flickered and played and swam around the ceiling. The Emperor was seated—almost sprawled—on the large hassock at the edge of the ballroom floor, staring raptly up at those patterns.

Nearby were three Starkiens, carrying rods and wearing power bands. Vhotan was some twenty feet away from the Emperor, standing over a table surface patterned with studs.

Except that he was not seated, his position and actions were very much like those Jim had seen in him once before.

With the appearance of the four people, the three Starkiens had automatically drawn their rods. Vhotan looked sharply up, caught sight of Slothiel, and waved the rods back into their belt loops. He turned from the table surface to face the group, scowling a little at Jim.

"I wasn't notified your Ten-units had returned to quarters," he said to Jim. "I can use those men right now."

"That's why I ordered them not to return to quarters," answered Jim.

Vhotan frowned sharply.

"What do you mean?" he said sharply. "And who gave you the authority to—"

He was interrupted by the sudden appearance of a servant—a man of the same appearance of Melness, carrying a small white box.

"This has just been delivered for you, Vhotan," the servant said. "It was sent through the Princess Afuan from the Governor of—" The servant gave the imperial name for Alpha Centauri.

"All right," scowled Vhotan. The servant disappeared. Vhotan carried the box over to his table service, felt about it for a second, and then lifted off a cover. His scowl deepened.

"What is this?" he asked. He started to

swing back to face them, but at that moment a new voice interrupted him.

"Why, it's Oran," said the voice. It was the Emperor, woken from his gazing at the refulgent patterns of the ceiling, and now walking over to peer interestedly into the box. His hand went down and came up holding what looked like a chunk of granite, rough-cut, perhaps three inches in diameter. "And there's a note with it."

He picked up a card from the box and looked at it.

"It says, *'At the request of my good friend, Jim Keil,'*" said the Emperor, turning to face Vhotan and the group as he read, "*'this specimen of rock from his homeland, the planet Earth, as a souvenir for the High-born, Vhotan.'*"

The Emperor, smiling delightedly, lifted his eyes to Vhotan.

"It's a present for you, Vhotan," he said cheerfully, "from our ex-Wolfling, here! Here, you'd better take it!"

The Emperor tossed the rock to the older High-born, whose long hands went up automatically to catch it in midair.

Vhotan's right hand closed about the flying object, and instantly he was covered with a brilliant blue light—an eye-baffling light in which his outlines were distorted and altered from the human into something unclear, but heavy and thick-bodied, bestial.

The Emperor screamed, stumbling backward and throwing up both long-fingered hands to shield his face from the sight.

"Nephew—" It was the voice of Vhotan, but somehow distorted and mangled into a growling bass. He raised blue-dazzling, thick, pawlike arms of light and took a step toward the Emperor, protectively.

The Emperor screamed again and stumbled backward, almost falling over a hassock, but keeping to his feet. His heels rang on the bare floor beyond the lounge area. He flung up a long arm with finger pointing.

"The Blue Beast!" he screamed to his Starkiens. "Kill it! *Kill it!*"

If there was a hesitation on the part of the Starkiens, it was for less than a fraction of a second. At once the three rods were drawn and came up, and the blue-haloed figure of Vhotan, still stepping toward the Emperor with arms outstretched, was laced with white fire.

The figure slumped. The blue light went out. A small piece of reddish rock rolled unheeded across the carpeted floor of the lounge section. Silent and still, sprawled upon that same carpet, lay Vhotan, his face untouched, but his body and limbs almost dismembered by incredible burn-lines.

There was no more sound or movement in the room. The Emperor stood staring at Vhotan. He stared for a long moment before his face and eyes began to change.

"Uncle?" he said in a quavering, uncertain voice. "*Uncle?*"

Slowly he began to move toward Vhotan. As he got closer, his shoulders bowed, and his face twisted like a man undergoing some process of torture. Slowly he came up to Vhotan and stood over him. He gazed down into Vhotan's untouched face. For such a violent death, Vhotan's face was strangely serene. His eyes and mouth were closed; the muscles of his features were relaxed. From the neck up he looked like someone engaged in a moment's silent meditation or thought.

"Vhotan . . ." began the Emperor on a note of anguish. But then his voice died in him, like the voice of a talking doll which had run down. He froze, unmoving, in the position in which he was, leaning over Vhotan, his arms half-reaching down toward the body of the older man. For a moment, to Jim, it seemed impossible that such a pose could be maintained. But the Emperor stayed as he was, as unmoving as a statue cast in plaster of paris.

Behind Jim, Slothiel stirred. He stepped forward toward the Emperor.

"Oran!" Slothiel said.

There was sudden amused laughter at the far end of the ballroom floor. Out of the corner of his eye, Jim caught sight of the three Starkiens spinning about swiftly, their rods coming up.

Then there were three odd, coughing sounds; and as Jim finished raising his head, he saw the three Starkiens stumble and fall.

On the polished ballroom floor, they lay as still as Vhotan lay.

Jim turned to look toward the far end of the polished floor. There, just in front of one of the green curtains, stood Galyan, holding a black rod in his right hand, and a strange, handgun sort of device, with a long, twisted barrel, in his left. Behind Galyan were Melness and Afuan. As Jim caught sight of them, Galyan tossed the handgun contemptuously away from him. It skidded across the polished floor until its further progress was blocked by a leg of one of the dead Starkiens.

Followed by Melness and Afuan, Galyan walked toward the lounge end of the room. His heels rapped with a strange loudness on the polished surface of the floor. He laughed again at the small group still standing there, as he came.

"You're quite a problem, Wolfling," he said to Jim. "Not only do you come back alive, but, having come back, you force me into taking action ahead of schedule. But it's all come out all right."

He reached the end of the polished floor and stepped onto the carpet. He stopped and transferred his gaze from Jim to Slothiel.

"No, Slothiel," he said mockingly. "Not 'Oran.'—'Galyan.' We will have to teach you to say 'Galyan.' "

Chapter 10

Galyan's words seemed to echo all about them. Looking at Slothiel, Jim saw the other High-born begin to stiffen and straighten. Galyan was the tallest of the High-born that Jim had seen, with the exception of the Emperor himself. But Slothiel was almost as tall. And now that he abandoned his carefully indifferent slouch, it could be seen how tall he was. The two men, both well over seven feet, faced each other across a distance of perhaps a dozen feet of carpeting.

"You've never been able to teach me anything, Galyan," said Slothiel in a dry, hard voice. "If I were you, I wouldn't expect to begin now."

"Slothiel, don't be an idiot!" Afuan spoke up. But Galyan cut her short.

"Never mind!" he said sharply, his lemon-yellow eyes still glittering unmovingly on Slothiel. "Who are we to tell Slothiel what to do? As he said—we've never been able to teach him anything."

"We?" Slothiel smiled bitterly. "Are you

into the Emperor's second person plural already, Galyan?"

"Did I say—*we?*" responded Galyan. "A slip of the tongue, Slothiel."

"Then you don't intend to kill him?" said Slothiel, indicating the frozen figure of the Emperor with a slight movement of his head.

"Kill him?" said Galyan. "Of course not. Care for him—that's what I'm going to do. Vhotan never did take the best care of him. He's not well, you know."

"Are you?" asked Jim.

Galyan's eyes flickered for a moment to Jim.

"Be patient, little Wolfling," Galyan purred. "Your time is coming. Right now I'm amusing myself with Slothiel."

"Amusing yourself?" said Slothiel with a grim irony that matched the cruel humor in Galyan's voice. "You'd better be thinking up explanations for how Vhotan died."

"I?" chuckled Galyan. "The Emperor's Starkiens killed Vhotan, at the Emperor's order. You saw that."

"And who killed the Starkiens?" said Slothiel.

"You, of course," said Galyan. "You went out of your head at the sight of Vhotan ordered killed for no reason—"

"No reason?" echoed Slothiel. "What about that disguised blue distortion light? Jim never had the Alpha Centauran Governor send it to Vhotan. That was your doing."

Galyan twitched a finger. Melness scuttled forward and sideways, to pick up the small granitic-looking shape from the carpet and tuck it into a pocket in his kilt. He retreated hastily behind Galyan again.

"What distortion light?" asked Galyan.

"I see," said Slothiel. He took a deep breath. "But of course I didn't kill the Starkiens."

"I wouldn't go around telling the other High-born that, if I were you," said Galyan. "The Emperor will need someone to look after him; now that Vhotan's dead, I'll be taking our uncle's place. If you go around telling a wild story like that, the Emperor may well decide that you need treatment and isolation for your own good."

"Oh? But even if I say nothing," drawled Slothiel, "those three Starkiens were killed by a heavy-duty intersperser. The other Starkiens, when they get back, will wonder how three of their number could have been killed by a rod while those three were wearing full power bands. I can prove that I haven't been near the heavy-duty weapon armory for years."

"No doubt," said Galyan. "But you said, 'when the other Starkiens get back.' You see, they won't be back."

Slothiel looked about suddenly at Jim. Jim nodded.

"So the Wolfling brought back word of our little traps on the colony planets, did he?" said the voice of Galyan. Both Jim and Slothiel looked back at the tall High-born.

"You know then, Slothiel. The Starkiens won't be back. I've got it in mind to create some new Starkiens—some responsible to me rather than to the Emperor. At any rate, you see your own choice. Be silent—or be removed from the social scene."

Slothiel laughed, and reaching over, drew the rod from the loops in Adok's belt.

Galyan laughed also, but with a half-incredulous note of contempt in his voice.

"Have you really lost your senses, Slothiel?" he said. "We've fenced as boys. You've got fast reflexes, but you know that no one's faster than I am. Except—" He nodded at the still-paralyzed figure of the Emperor.

"But we haven't tried it as men," said Slothiel. "Besides, I'm a little tired of all our play-acting here on the Throne World. I think I'd like to kill you."

He took a step forward. Galyan stepped hastily back onto the polished surface of the ballroom floor and slowly drew the rod from the loops in his own belt.

"Shall we bet on it?" he said. "Let's bet a banishment amount of Lifetime Points, Slothiel. How about fifty Lifetime Points? That ought to put either one of us over the limit."

"Don't talk to me of toys," said Slothiel, slowly advancing foot after foot, as Galyan equally slowly backed and circled away from him. "I think I've lost my taste for gambling. I want something a little more exciting."

They were almost in the center of the polished floor area now. There was still a dozen feet between them, but tall and bent over as they were, their wide shoulders hunched forward, the rods held low before them, it seemed as if scarcely one of their own long arm lengths separated the two of them.

Abruptly the rod in Slothiel's hand spouted the white lightning of its charge. At the same time, he leaned back and to one side in an attempt to outflank Galyan.

Galyan, however, crouched under the white bolt, which crackled where his head had been a moment before, and spun on his heels, still in crouched position, to come up facing Slothiel and with his own rod shooting white fire.

A little faster, and Galyan would have been able to drive the fire of his own rod under the line of fire from Slothiel's rod. However, the moment of Galyan's turning was enough time to allow Slothiel to lower the aim of his own weapon, so that the discharge from Galyan's rod met the discharge from Slothiel's head on, and the two lines of white fire splashed harmlessly into an aurora of sparks. From that first moment, the lines of fire from the two rods were never disengaged.

Following the first wild gamble by both men (and Jim had practiced at the rods enough with Adok to understand what gambles they had been)—Slothiel's attack and

Galyan's counter—both of the High-born fought defensively and warily for more than a dozen fairly routine engages. As Jim had discovered with Adok, fighting with the rods was very similar to fencing with sabers, provided they were sabers that changed lengths frequently and unexpectedly. The focal point of the fire put forth by the rods— that point at which the discharge was most destructive—was at the tip of an inner cone of pure white light, and this cone could be extended by the man holding the rod, at will, from a length of six inches to ten feet. This was the point at which the utmost power of the rod was exerted. Directly in counter, the point of the cone of fire in one rod could be blocked only by the point of the cone of fire in another. However, if the cone tip should miss its target and the opposing rod could project its cone tip into the stream of fire behind the other tip, the penetrative cone could be bent aside, so that the attacking cone could go on to strike its target.

It was not just a matter of deflecting the stream of fire from the opponent's rod, therefore, but of deflecting it with a portion of your own flame, which was stronger than that part of the opponent's flame it encountered.

Slothiel and Galyan moved about the polished floor, each careful to avoid being backed against one of the green-draperied walls. From the encounters of their weapons came a steady succession of spark showers—exploding suddenly into near-fountains of light when the two cone points were the parts of the flames to make contact. Galyan was smiling grimly, thin-lipped and narrow-nostriled. Slothiel, on the other hand, after his first savage attack, fought with a sort of dreamy grace and a relaxed face, as if this were not a duel to the death but some minor sporting engagement in which he had perhaps backed himself with a small bet.

But Slothiel's apparent indifference was no true clue to the way in which the duel was progressing. Hardly more than a few weeks ago, it would have looked to Jim more like some smoothly expert dance by two large men with some sort of Roman candles in their hands—a dance intended to demonstrate the rhythm of the men and the beauty of the fireworks rather than anything else. Now, he knew better. Moreover, because he knew better, he was able to see that the duel could have only one ending. As graceful and swift as Slothiel was, half a dozen times already Galyan had almost caught him on the disengage from an encounter of the cone tips of their weapons. Sooner or later Slothiel's luck and skill would not prevent him from being a little bit too slow in deflecting the other man's fire.

Galyan was, indeed, the quicker of the two. And in this sort of duel, that meant everything.

In fact, as they all watched, the end came. Galyan leaped to his left suddenly, struck high with his flame, dropped down under the line of Slothiel's countering discharge, and flicked up again inside to slash across Slothiel's left thigh and left upper arm, which held the rod.

Slothiel went down on the polished floor on his right knee, his left arm dangling. His rod dropped and skidded a little way across the floor.

He laughed up into the face of Galyan.

"You find it funny, do you?" panted Galyan. "I'll wipe that smile off your face!"

Galyan lifted his rod to bring it down across Slothiel's features.

"Galyan!" shouted Jim, running forward.

The sound of his voice did not stop Galyan, but the rapid beating of Jim's shoes upon the polished floor did. Galyan whirled like a cat.

Jim had drawn the rod from his own belt as he ran. He had just time to get it up and send the flame lancing from it, ahead of him, before Galyan's rod joined its discharge with his in a shower of sparks.

Jim broke the flames of both rods high, disengaged, and stepped back. Galyan laughed.

"Wolfling, Wolfling . . ." he said, shaking his head. "You never really have learned what High-born means, have you? It seems I'll have to give you a lesson?"

"Jim!" called Slothiel from the floor behind Galyan. "Don't do it! You haven't got a chance! Run!"

"You're both wrong," said Jim. Now that he was actually engaged with Galyan, his mind was as cold as ice, and the remote coldness of his voice echoed that iciness within him.

He engaged with Galyan, and they fought through at least a dozen engage-and-disengage actions. Galyan's eyebrows rose.

"Not bad at all," he said. "In fact, very good for anyone not a High-born—and unthinkably good for a wild man. I do hate to waste you, Wolfling."

Jim did not answer. He continued to fight on, warily and conservatively, concerned only with keeping the cone tip of the discharge from Galyan's weapon always out beyond the cone tip of his own flame and making sure he would not be backed against one of the walls. If he had not had experience fencing with foil, épée, and saber back on Earth, he would never have been able to pick up enough of the technique of handling the rods in the few short weeks in which he had trained with Adok. But that experience, combined with his own native ability, was now paying off. Little by little, as the duel went on, he found himself making his moves more surely.

"In fact, why should I waste you?" panted Galyan during one of the engages in which their faces came within a few feet of each other. The white skin of the High-born's features gleamed with perspiration. "Be sensible, Wolfling, and don't make me kill you. Slothiel has to die anyway—now. But I had large plans for you, as head of my own, new Starkiens."

Jim maintained his silence. But he stepped up the pressure of his attack. Off to one side, without warning, he heard the sound of running feet on the bare floor, and Ro's voice shouting.

"Keep back!"

Jim dared not look up at the moment, but a few seconds later he found himself facing toward the lounge end of the room, and he caught a quick glimpse of Ro, standing beside the fallen Slothiel, holding the rod Slothiel had dropped, and covering Afuan with it. Melness lay sprawled at Adok's feet, and it looked as if the master servant's neck had been broken. Only the unmoving figure of the Emperor, standing over the dead Vhotan, was unchanged.

"Who do you think you are?" snarled Galyan suddenly. "When I speak to you, I want an answer, Wolfling!"

Jim countered a high thrust from the taller figure and stepped to the left in a disengage, without a word.

"All right!" said Galyan, showing his teeth in an almost mechanical smile. "I've had enough of this! I've been playing with you, hoping you'd come to your senses. Now I'm through with that. I'm going to kill you, Wolfling!"

The High-born attacked suddenly, in a shower of sparks, and Jim found himself fighting for his life. Galyan had a tremendous advantage in reach over him, and the taller man was using that reach, as well as the spring in his long legs, to the upmost advantage. Parrying swiftly and continuously, Jim was still forced to give ground. He backed away, and Galyan crowded close upon him, driving him still further backward. Jim attempted to circle to the right, but found that way cut off by the blazing white lightning of Galyan's weapon. He tried to break to the left, but Galyan outreached him. Out of the corners of his eyes he could see the other walls of the room, and from their distances he knew that the fourth wall must be close behind him. If Galyan could pin him against the wall, the restriction of Jim's movements would give the High-born an advantage that would end the duel quickly.

Galyan's teeth were bared fixedly now, and sweat dripped from his chin. His great advantage in reach cut off any escape to right or left. Shortly, also, there would be no possible retreat straight backward for Jim.

There was only one way out of this prison of flame with which Galyan was fencing him about. That was to outdo Galyan at the High-born's strongest point. Jim must counter Galyan's attack with an attack of his own, which would force Galyan first to

halt, then to retreat in his turn. And in such
an attack, there could be only one counter
to Galyan's advantage in reach—and that
was speed. Jim would have to be quicker
than the High-born.

There was no point in further hesitation.
Jim came out of a disengage and attacked
savagely. At the first fury of Jim's onslaught,
Galyan gave ground along three steps out
of sheer, reflexive surprise. But then he stood
his ground.

He laughed hoarsely, pantingly, and briefly. He seemed about to say something, but
evidently decided against wasting his breath,
of which neither he nor Jim had any to
spare. For better than a dozen engages and
disengages they stood essentially toe to toe
on the gleaming floor, neither one giving an
inch.

It was a murderous pace, one that neither
man could keep up for another minute without dropping from exhaustion and breath-
lessness. But Jim did not slacken off, and
slowly Galyan's eyes began to widen. He
stared at Jim across the twin, clashing
streams of fire, through the showers of white
sparks.

"You—can't—do—" he gasped.

"I am—" panted Jim.

Galyan's face unexpectedly contorted into
a staring mask of fury. He disengaged from
Jim's current attack and went immediately
into a sweeping circle with the fire from his

instrument—almost the type of maneuver that singlestick fighters call a *moulinet*.

It was a simple, raw bid to outspeed the cone tip of flame from Jim's weapon. If Galyan could get ahead of that guarding cone tip, he would have a fraction of a second in which to go back in over Jim's guard and destroy him. Galyan's flame whipped over and down, and Jim's blurred along with it. For a full arc, the desperate race held, without Galyan's weapon gaining—and then, it was Jim whose cone tip moved ahead.

He gained, coming up on the second arc, broke in over the line of Galyan's weapon, and shot the full force of his flame into the taller man's unprotected chest.

Galyan tottered and fell, his own weapon coming around and down, to tap its rod end against Jim's right side just below the ribs before falling from his hand to the floor. Jim felt a sudden coldness and hollowness inside him. Then Galyan was slumped at his feet.

Jim lifted his head slowly, his lungs pumping heavily to restore oxygen to his exhausted body.

He saw, through sweat-blurred eyes, that Slothiel now held the rod that Ro had held earlier, covering Afuan. Not only that, but Slothiel was, amazingly, back on his feet, although he leaned heavily on Ro. As soon as he had breath left to spare for walking,

Jim moved slowly from Galyan's dead body over toward Ro and Slothiel.

"Jim . . ." said Slothiel wonderingly, looking at him and slowly putting the rod he held back into his belt. Now he ignored Afuan, as Jim came up, "what are you?"

"A Wolfling," said Jim. "What're you doing back on your feet?"

Slothiel laughed, not entirely cheerfully.

"We heal fast, with the help of our power sources, we High-born," he said. "How about you?"

"I'll do," said Jim. He kept his right elbow pressed close against his side. "But I've left another body for you to clean up. I think it's time for me to go home."

"Home?" Slothiel echoed.

"Back to Earth—the world I came from," said Jim. "The more thoroughly this is hushed up, the better for the Emperor. Nobody will miss me if I disappear, and you can tell the other High-born that Galyan killed Vhotan and the Starkiens in a fit of madness, and you had to kill him in return to protect the Emperor."

He glanced over at Afuan, who stood like a tall, white statue.

"That is," Jim said, "if you can persuade the Princess to keep quiet."

Slothiel looked at her only briefly.

"Afuan won't disagree with me," Slothiel said. "Galyan suggested that if I didn't agree with him, the Emperor might decide I needed isolation and treatment. The same can apply to her."

He turned, letting go of Ro, and walked, a little limpingly but completely under his own power, off the polished floor onto the carpet and up to the unmoving figure of the Emperor. Jim and Ro followed him.

Slothiel touched the Emperor lightly on the arm.

"Oran . . ." he said gently.

For a moment the Emperor did not move. Then, slowly, he straightened and turned about, breaking into a warm smile as he did so.

"Slothiel!" he said. "Good of you to come so quickly. Did you know that I can't find Vhotan anywhere? He was here just a few minutes ago, and I could swear he hadn't left the room, but he's vanished completely."

The Emperor looked down the long length of the polished floor, around the draperied walls, back up and around the lounge, at the carpet, and at the ceiling, over which the colored shapes still played. He looked everywhere but at the still shape down at his feet.

"You know, I had a dream, Slothiel," the Emperor went on, wistfully looking back at the other High-born. "It was just last night— or at least, it was some time recently. I dreamed that Vhotan was dead, Galyan was dead, and all my Starkiens were dead. And when I went looking around the palace and the Throne World to find the other High-born to tell them about this, there was no one—not in the palace, not on the whole world. I was all alone. You don't think I would ever be left alone like that, do you, Slothiel?"

"Not while I'm alive, Oran," said Slothiel.

"Thank you, Slothiel," said the Emperor. He looked around the room again, however, and his voice became a little fretful. "But I wish I knew what happened to Vhotan. Why isn't he here?"

"He had to go away for a while, Oran," said Slothiel. "He told me to stay with you until he gets back."

The Emperor's face lit up once more with his warm smile.

"Well, then, everything's all right!" he said happily. He threw an arm around Slothiel's shoulders and looked around the room. "Why, there's Afuan—and little Ro and our little Wolfling. Ex-Wolfling, I should say."

He gazed at Jim, and his smile slowly faded into a solemn, rather sad expression.

"You're going away, aren't you—Jim?" he said, plainly dredging up the name from some hidden corner of his memory. "I thought I heard you say something about that just now."

"Yes, Oran," said Jim. "I have to go now."

The Emperor nodded, his face still sadly solemn.

"Yes, I heard it, all right," he said, half to himself. His eyes fastened on Jim. "I hear things sometimes, you know, even when I'm not really listening. And I understand things, too; sometimes I understand them better than any of the other High-born. It's a good thing you're going back to your own world, Jim."

The Emperor's hand slipped from Slothiel's shoulder. He took a step forward and stood looking down at Jim.

"You're full of young energy out there, Jim," he said. "And we're tired here. Very tired, sometimes. It's going to be all right for you and your Wolflings, Jim. I can see it, you know—very often I see things like that, quite clearly...."

His lemon-yellow eyes seemed to cloud, going a little out of focus, so that he stared through Jim rather than at him.

"I've seen you doing well, Jim," he said. "You and the other Wolflings. And what's well for you is well for all—all of us." His eyes unclouded, and once more he was focused on Jim again. "Something tells me you've done me a signal service, Jim. I think before you go, I'd like to finish your adoption. Yes, from now on I declare you to be a High-born, Jim Keil." He laughed, a little, suddenly. "... I'm not giving you anything you don't already have."

He straightened up and turned back to Slothiel.

"What should I do now?" he asked Slothiel.

"I think you should send Afuan back to

her quarters now," said Slothiel, "and tell her that she's to stay there until she hears something more from you."

"Yes." The Emperor's glance swung around to fasten on Afuan, but she met it for only a moment, before turning furiously upon Jim and Ro, who stood beside him.

"Mud-face! Wild man!" she spat. "Crawl off into the bushes and mate!"

Jim stiffened, but Ro caught hold of his left arm.

"No!" she said, almost proudly. "You don't need to. Don't you see—she's jealous! Jealous of *me!*"

Still holding strongly to his arm, she looked up into his face.

"I'm going with you, Jim," she said. "Back to this world of yours."

"Yes," said the Emperor unexpectedly but thoughtfully, "that's right. I saw it that way. Yes, little Ro should go with him. . . ."

"Afuan!" said Slothiel sharply.

The Princess threw him a glance as full of hatred as the one she had directed at Ro and Jim. She disappeared.

Jim's head swam suddenly. He took a strong grip on himself internally, and the room steadied about him.

"We have to go quickly, then," he said. "I'll send you those Starkiens from my ship, Slothiel. You can keep them close to the Emperor until you're able to get back as many as possible of the other units who've been sent out to the Colony Worlds. If you order them back quickly, you shouldn't lose too many of them to Galyan's antimatter traps."

"I'll do that. Good-bye, Jim," said Slothiel. "And thank you."

"Good-bye, Jim," said the Emperor. He stepped forward, offering his hand. Jim freed his left arm from Ro's grasp and took the long fingers awkwardly with his own left hand.

"Adok," said the Emperor, without letting go of Jim's hand, but glancing over at the Starkien, "do you have a family?"

"No more, Oran," answered Adok in his usual flat tone. "My son is grown, and my wife has gone back to the women's compound."

"Would you like to go with Jim?" asked the Emperor.

"I—" For the first time since Jim had known him, the Starkien seemed at a loss for words. "I am not experienced in liking or not liking, Oran."

"If I order you to go with Jim and Ro, and stay with them for the rest of your life," said the Emperor, "will you go willingly?"

"Yes, Oran. Willingly," said Adok.

The Emperor let go of Jim's hand.

"You'll need Adok," he said to Jim.

"Thank you, Oran," said Jim.

Ro's grip tightened on his arm once more.

"Good-bye, Oran. Good-bye, Slothiel," said Ro. And at once they were no longer in the palace room, but at the docking berth where Jim had left the ship containing his Ten-units of Starkiens.

Harn was standing just outside the ship, like a man on watch, when they appeared. He turned quickly to face Jim.

"It's good to see you, sir," he said.

Jim unexpectedly felt ship and berthing dock waver and slip around him once more. He pulled himself back to clearheadedness again just in time to hear Adok speaking to Harn.

"The High-born Vhotan and the Prince Galyan are dead," Adok was saying quickly; "and three Starkiens have been killed. The High-born Slothiel has taken Vhotan's place. You and your men are to go to the Emperor."

"Yes," Jim managed to say.

"Sir!" acknowledged Harn, and vanished.

Abruptly they were inside the ship, Jim, Ro, and Adok. Another wave of disorientation passed through Jim, and he felt Ro helping him down gently onto the level surface of a hassocklike bed.

"What is it—Adok!" He heard her voice, but distantly, as if at the far end of a tilted corridor, down which he was sliding, ever faster, ever farther away from her. He made a great effort, and visualized in his mind, first, the spaceport at Alpha Centauri III, and then, from there, the spaceport back on Earth from which he had taken off. It was his last effort—from now on it would be up to the ship. But from what he had read out of the Files of the Throne World's learning centers, he had no doubt the ship would be able to locate Earth from the directions he had just given it.

He let go, and went back to sliding away down the tilted corridor. But there was one thing more yet he had to do. He fought his way back to consciousness and Ro for a second.

"Galyan burned my side as he died," he muttered to her. "Now I'm dying. So you'll have to tell them for me, Ro. On Earth. Tell them . . . everything. . . ."

"But you won't die!" Ro was crying, holding him fiercely with both her arms about him. "You won't die . . . you *won't*. . . ."

But even as she held him, he slipped out of her grasp and went sliding—this time with no further check or hope of return— down that long tilted corridor into the utter darkness.

Chapter 11

When Jim opened his eyes at last to light after that long slide into darkness, it took him a long time with the help of the light to recognize the shapes of things around him. He felt as if he had been dead for years. Gradually, however, vision sharpened. Perception returned. He became aware that he lay on his back on a surface harder than any hassock; and the ceiling he stared up at was white, but oddly grainy and close above him.

With a great effort he managed to turn his head, and saw shapes that he gradually made out to be a small bedside table, several chairs, and a white screen of the sort used in hospitals. In all, a single room, with a window at the far end that let in a yellow, summer sunlight he had not seen for quite a while. Through the window he could see only sky, blue sky, with a few isolated puffs of white clouds scattered about it. He lay staring at the sky, slowly trying to put things together.

Obviously he was on Earth. That meant

that at least five days must have passed
while he was unconscious. But if he was on
Earth, what was he doing here? Where was
here? And where were Ro and Adok, to say
nothing of the ship?—All this, leaving aside
the fact that he seemed to be alive, when he
had certainly seemed to have had no right
to be so.

He lay still, thinking. After a little while,
absently, he felt the side where the flame of
Galyan's torch had penetrated as the High-
born had died. But his side felt smooth and
well. Interested, he pulled down the covers,
pulled up the blue pajama top he seemed to
be wearing, and examined that side. As far
as he could see, it looked as if he had never
been wounded at all.

He pulled the covers up again and lay
back. He felt well, if a little heavy-bodied,
as if the lassitude of a long sleep were still
clinging to him. He turned his head and
looked at the small table by his bedside. It
held an insulating plastic pitcher, a glass
with some remnants of ice floating at the
top of the water within it, and a small box
of paper handkerchiefs. The signs were overwhelming that he was in a hospital. This
would not be surprising if he still had the
deep wound in his side that Galyan's rod
had made. But there was no wound.

He investigated further. Below the top
level of the table by his bed was a vertical
surface with a telephone handset clinging
magnetically to it. He picked up the hand-

set and listened, but there was no dial tone. Experimentally he tried dialing some numbers on the dial set in the center of the inner face of the handset. But the phone remained dead. He put it back, and in the process of doing so, discovered a button on the vertical surface.

He pressed the button.

Nothing happened. After about five minutes of waiting, he pressed it again.

This time, it was only a matter of seconds before the door swung open. A man entered—a heavy-bodied young man not much shorter than himself, with a thick, powerful-looking body dressed in white slacks and white jacket. He came up to the bed, looked down at Jim without a word, and reached to the bed to take Jim's left wrist. Lifting the wrist, he counted the pulse, gazing at his wristwatch as he did so.

"Yes, I'm alive," Jim told him. "What hospital is this?"

The male nurse, as he seemed to be, made a noncommittal sound in his throat. Finished counting, he dropped Jim's wrist back onto the bed and turned toward the door.

"Hold on!" said Jim, sitting up suddenly.

"Just lie there!" said the man in a deep, gruff voice. Hastily he opened the door and went out, slamming it slightly behind him.

Jim threw back the covers and jumped out of bed in the same quick motion. He took three steps to the door and grasped its handle. But his fingers slipped around the smooth, immovable metal as he tried to turn it. It was locked.

He shook the handle once and then stepped back. His first impulse—quenched almost as soon as it was born by the immediate caution of his now thoroughly awakened mind—was to pound on the door until someone came. Now, instead, he stood gazing at it thoughtfully.

This place was beginning to look less like a hospital and more like a place of care for the violently insane. He spun about quickly and went to the window. What he saw confirmed the growing suspicion in him of his surroundings. Invisible from his bed, a mesh of fine wire covered the window opening completely, some four inches beyond the window itself. The wire looked relatively thin, but it was undoubtedly strong enough to be escape-proof for anyone lacking tools.

Jim looked out the window and down, but what he saw gave him little information—merely a width of green lawn bordered on all sides by tall pine trees. The trees were tall enough to cut off the view of whatever lay beyond them.

Jim turned around and thoughtfully went back to sit down on the edge of his bed. After a moment he lay down and pulled the covers up over him again.

With the patience that was so much an innate part of him, he waited.

At least a couple of hours must have gone by before anything more happened. Then, without any advance notice, the door to his room opened and the male nurse came back in, followed by a slight man in his late forties or early fifties with a balding head and narrow face, wearing a white physician's coat. They came up to the head of the bed together, and the slight man in the white physician's coat met Jim's eyes.

"Well, all right," he said, turning his head slightly toward the male nurse. "I won't need you."

The male nurse went out, clicking the door shut behind him. The physician, for such he certainly must be, reached out for Jim's wrist and took his pulse as the other man had done earlier.

"Yes," he said, as if to himself, after a moment. He dropped the wrist, pulled back the covers, lifted the pajama coat, and examined Jim's side—the one that had been wounded. His fingers probed here and there. Abruptly Jim stiffened.

"Sore?" the physician asked.

"Yes," said Jim flatly.

"Well, that's interesting," said the doctor. "—if true."

"Doctor," said Jim quietly. "Is there something wrong with you?—Or with me?"

"No, there's nothing wrong with you," said the physician, yanking Jim's pajama top down and tossing the covers up on him again. "As for me—I don't believe it. The only thing I believe is what I saw when you

came in here—and that was a small perforation in your right side."

"What is it you don't believe, then?" asked
Jim.

"I don't believe that you had a burned
area where that perforation was, a burned
area at least two inches wide and six inches
deep, six days ago," said the physician. "Yes,
I've seen the pictures of your ship on tele-
vision, and I know what that tall girl told
me, but I don't believe it. In the first place,
with that kind of damage done to you
internally, you'd be dead long before you
got here. Now, I can believe in a small perforation that heals without a visible scar.
But I can't swallow the larger story."

"Is there any reason you should?" asked
Jim gently.

"No, there isn't," said the physician. "So
I'm not going to worry about it. As far as
I'm concerned, you're well and ready for
anything—and I'll so advise them."

"Who's them?" asked Jim.

The physician stared down at him.

"Doctor," said Jim quietly, "for some reason you seem to have a bad opinion of me.
That's your privilege. But I don't think it's
your privilege to keep a patient in the dark—
not only about where he is, but about who
it is who are evidently concerned with him.
You mentioned a tall girl who told you about
me. Is she outside right now?"

"No, she isn't," said the physician. "As
for answering your question, the people who

are concerned with you are officials of the world government. And I've been told that it's my duty not to talk to you except as required in your treatment. You don't require any more treatment, and so I've got no more excuse to talk to you."

He turned and headed for the door. With his hand on the knob, he seemed to experience a twinge of conscience, for he paused and turned back to Jim.

"They'll be sending someone in to see you shortly after I tell them you're well," he said. "You'll be able to ask him all the questions you like."

He turned away from Jim once more, tried the door, and found it locked. He pounded on it with his fist and shouted through it to someone who was evidently on the far side. After a moment the door was cautiously unlocked, and he was allowed to slip out through the least possible opening. The door slammed and clicked shut once more.

The wait was considerably shorter this time. It was no more than fifteen or twenty minutes before the door opened again—and immediately clicked shut once more—behind a man about ten years younger than the physician, with a brown, tanned face and a gray business suit. He came in, nodded unsmilingly at Jim, and briskly drew one of the chairs up to the bed. Jim sat up on the edge of the bed.

"I'm Daniel Wylcoxin," the man said. "Call me Dan, if you like. There's going to be a

Government Committee Inquiry, and I've been assigned as your counsel."

"What if I don't want you?" asked Jim mildly.

"Then, of course, you don't have to have me," said Wylcoxin. "Actually, the Inquiry has nothing to do with a court trial. That's to come later, if the Inquiry decides to take that course of action. Actually, you don't legally need counsel, and if you don't want me, I'm not going to be forced on you. On the other hand, it's not likely the Committee would recognize someone else as counsel for you, since—as I say—counsel really isn't supposed to be necessary for you."

"I see," said Jim. "I'd like to ask a few questions."

"Fire away," said Wylcoxin, leaning back in his chair and laying his arms flat on the armrests of it.

"Where am I?" asked Jim bluntly.

"That, I'm afraid, I can't tell you," said Wylcoxin. "This is a government hospital for special people and situations where secrecy is required. I was brought here in a closed car myself. *I* don't know where we are, except that we're no more than twenty minutes' ride from Government Center, where my own office is."

"Where's my spaceship? And where are the woman and the man who came with me?"

"Your ship is at Government Center spaceport," said Wylcoxin, "surrounded by security guards that keep everyone at a quarter-mile distance. Your two companions are still aboard the ship—for which you can thank the Governor of Alpha Centauri III. He's here on Earth, and when government people wanted to move your two friends out and put their own men aboard the ship, the Governor evidently talked them out of it. It seems the woman you have with you is what they call a High-born, and the Governor is evidently scared silly of anyone in that classification. I suppose I can't blame him—"

Wylcoxin broke off to look curiously at Jim.

"I understand the High-born run the Empire?" he wound up.

"They do," said Jim flatly. "What am I doing here?"

"This lady, this High-born—"

"Her name is Ro," interrupted Jim grimly.

"Ro, then," said Wylcoxin, "met the first government people to come aboard your spaceship after it landed. There was quite a well-known group, I understand, because the Alpha Centauri Governor, who's visiting Government Center here, recognized the ship as being one belonging to these High-born. Anyway, Ro let them aboard and told them quite a story, including how you got wounded fighting some kind of duel with a Prince of the Empire. She said you were a lot better, but she didn't object when the government offered to take you to one of our own hospitals for care. Evidently they convinced her that whatever she could do, the kind of medicine you were used to might do you more good in the long run."

"Yes," murmured Jim. "She's not the suspicious kind."

"Evidently," said Wylcoxin. "At any rate, she let them take you. And here you are. And the Committee's scheduled to start its Inquiry as soon as you're well enough to appear before it. I understand the doctor's already certified you in that respect, so the proceedings will probably start tomorrow morning."

"What are they inquiring about?" asked Jim.

"Well ..." Wylcoxin leaned forward in his chair. "That's the point. As I say, the Inquiry has no relation to any court procedure. Theoretically it's called simply to supply the government with information, so that it will know how to act about you, your friends, and your ship. Actually, and I imagine you expected something like this, it's merely a get-together to determine if there's any reason why they shouldn't set the wheels in motion to bring you to trial for treason."

The final words of Wylcoxin's sentence fell softly on the still air of the hospital room. Jim looked at him for a second.

"You said I 'expected' it?" Jim echoed quietly. "What makes you think I expected something like this when I got back here?"

"Why"—Wylcoxin paused and shot him a

keen glance—"Maxwell Holland came back after you left Alpha Centauri III for the Throne World with those other High-born, and evidently he reported you as saying then that you meant to pay no attention to your orders, but to raise any kind of hell you felt like raising at the Imperial Court. Certainly Holland is going to testify to that effect tomorrow before the Committee. Didn't you say what he says you said?"

"No," said Jim. "I said I'd have to follow my own judgment from there on."

"That might sound like the same thing to the Committee," said Wylcoxin.

"It sounds," said Jim, "like this Committee has already made up its mind to consider me guilty of—what was it—treason?"

"I'd say they have," said Wylcoxin. "But then, I'm automatically on your side of it. And your side of it doesn't look too good from where I sit. You were carefully selected to be the man sent in to the Throne World, and trained at a great deal of trouble and expense, so that you could go among these High-born and observe them. Then you were to report back to Earth with your observations, so government could make up its mind whether we were really a lost bit of this Empire, and bound to consider ourselves a part of it, or whether there was a chance we'd evolved on Earth here entirely separately—and really were a different race entirely from the so-called human beings of the Empire. Right?"

"Yes, that's right," said Jim.

"Good, so far," said Wylcoxin. "But now, according to this Ro, instead of merely observing, you started out by getting into a fight with one of the High-born and knifing him aboard the ship going to the Throne World, then followed that up by joining some military bodyguard belonging to the Emperor when you got there, winding it all up by involving yourself in some kind of intrigue in which the Emperor's uncle and cousin were killed, as well as several bodyguards. Is *that* right?"

"It covers the physical facts of what happened," said Jim evenly, "but it distorts them, and the situations that gave rise to them, completely out of recognition."

"You're saying that this girl Ro is a liar?" Wylcoxin demanded.

"I'm saying that she didn't tell it that way," said Jim. "Tell me, did you get the story direct from her, or secondhand from somebody else who heard it from her?"

Wylcoxin sank thoughtfully back in his chair and rubbed his chin.

"I got it secondhand," he admitted. "But if the man who reported what she said to me can make it sound the way I made it sound just now to you, then that's the way government witnesses will be making it sound to the Committee tomorrow morning."

"It sounds more than ever like a hanging Committee," said Jim.

"Maybe. . . ." Wylcoxin rubbed his chin thoughtfully again. Suddenly he jumped to his feet and began to walk up and down the room.

"I'll tell you," he said, stopping in front of Jim. "I wasn't too happy about being assigned as your counsel. Maybe I'd been brainwashed a little myself."

He checked himself.

"I don't say that because so far you've said anything to make me alter my own feelings about you and the situation," he said hastily. "I say that simply because you've opened my eyes to the fact that there might—I say *might*—be a certain amount of prejudice on the other side."

He sat down again in his chair before Jim.

"Well," he said, "let's hear your side of it. What happened from the time you left Alpha Centauri III until you landed back here?"

"I got myself taken to the Throne World," said Jim, looking straight at the other man, "to find out, as you say, whether the Empire was populated by humans we were related to, or whether we were a separate stock from them entirely. Everything else happened after that as necessity dictated."

Wylcoxin sat for several seconds after Jim had stopped talking, almost as if he expected Jim to continue.

"Is that all you've got to say?" he demanded then.

"That's all for now," said Jim. "I'll tell a more complete story to that Committee tomorrow if they care to listen."

"You're deliberately not telling me anything you know that might help you, then," said Wylcoxin. "Don't you understand, I can't be of any use to you unless you're as open with me as you possibly can be?"

"I understand it," said Jim. "Quite frankly, I don't trust you. I trust your goodwill and honesty toward me, but I don't trust your capability to understand what I tell you, any more than I'd trust the capability of anyone else who hadn't been to the Throne World himself."

"Why, man," said Wylcoxin, "that takes in everyone on Earth!"

"That's right," said Jim. "I don't think anyone from Earth could help me much. Not if Max Holland, as you say, is there to testify against me, and the Committee seems determined to find grounds for bringing me to trial for treason."

"Then I can't be any good to you!"

Wylcoxin jumped to his feet out of the chair and headed toward the door.

"Wait a minute," said Jim. "Perhaps you can't help me by defending me, any more than any other Earth-born human can. But you can help me in other ways."

"How?" Wylcoxin turned almost belligerently, with one hand on the doorknob.

"To start off with," said Jim quietly, "by

considering me innocent until I'm proven guilty."

Wylcoxin stood for a second with his hand on the doorknob; then his hand dropped free. He came slowly back and sat down in the chair once more.

"My apologies," he said, looking up to Jim. "All right. You tell me what I can do."

"Well," said Jim, "for one thing, you can go to that Committee meeting with me tomorrow as my counsel. For another thing, you can answer a few questions. First—why should the Committee and the government and people in general be so eager to find me guilty of treason when all I've done is come back safe, with a valuable spaceship and a couple of people from the Throne World? I don't see how either of those things could suggest that I had treason in my heart when I was on the Throne World. Of course, there's Max Holland wanting to nail me. But if it was just him, it doesn't seem to me that I'd have too much to worry about."

"Why, don't you understand?" Wylcoxin frowned up at him. "All this talk of treason— all this is because they're afraid that you did things on the Throne World that will make the Empire want to take it out on Earth, in payment or revenge."

"Why?" asked Jim.

"Why . . ." Wylcoxin did not quite sputter, but he came close to it. "Maybe it's because of you that an uncle and a cousin of the Emperor are dead. Isn't it possible that this

Emperor would want to make somebody pay for those deaths?''

Jim chuckled. Wylcoxin's eyebrows rose in astonishment and bafflement.

"You think that's funny?" the other man demanded.

"No," said Jim. "It's just that I suddenly see where it all came from, this fear that has me threatened with a charge of treason. Treason carries the death penalty, doesn't it?''

"Sometimes . . ." said Wylcoxin, grudgingly. "But what're you talking about?"

"I'm afraid I couldn't explain it to you," said Jim. "Tell me, can you go and see Ro aboard the spaceship?"

Wylcoxin shook his head.

"I tried that earlier," he said. "The authorities wouldn't let me go out to the ship."

"Can you send her a message?" asked Jim.

"I think I can do that." Wylcoxin frowned. "I don't know if I can get an answer for you, though."

"An answer won't be necessary," said Jim. "Ro gave me up to Earth's doctors without any protest. So she must be trusting them, where I'm concerned. That leads me to believe that she doesn't know what this Committee is aiming at with me tomorrow. Could you get word to her of what they're after, and what their attitude toward me is likely to be?''

"I think so," said Wylcoxin. More energetically he added, "Yes, I know I can! If nothing else, I can get word to her when she comes in tomorrow morning. They'll be calling her to repeat her story to the Committee. She'll be there tomorrow too, undoubtedly."

"If you can get word to her this evening on the ship, I'd appreciate that more," said Jim.

"I should be able to." Wylcoxin looked at him oddly. "But what do you expect from her? She can't very well change her story from what it was earlier."

"I don't expect her to," said Jim.

"But you said no one from Earth could help you. That leaves only Ro and that other passenger you brought back from the Throne World," said Wylcoxin. "Let me warn you that these are almost in the position of being prosecution star witnesses. In short, you don't have anyone to testify for you."

"I might have." Jim smiled slightly. "There's the Governor of Alpha Centauri III."

"Him!" Wylcoxin's eyes lit up. "I'd never thought of him! That's right—he did put in a good word for your Ro when she wanted to stay aboard the spaceship. Maybe he would speak up in your defense tomorrow. . . . Want me to get in touch with him?"

Jim shook his head.

"No," he said. "Leave that to me."

Wylcoxin shook his head.

"I don't know," he said helplessly. "I just don't know. But I guess I'm along for the ride. Anything else?"

He looked up at Jim.

"No," said Jim. "Just get that message to Ro if you can."

"All right." Wylcoxin got to his feet. "I'll be around about half an hour before it's time for you to be taken into Government Center, and I'll ride in with you."

He went over to the door, rattled the doorknob, and pounded on the door panel.

"It's Wylcoxin!" he shouted through the door. "Let me out!"

After a second the door opened gingerly. Wylcoxin looked over at Jim.

"Well, good night," he said. "And good luck."

"Thank you," said Jim.

Wylcoxin went out, and the door was shut and locked behind him.

Jim lay down on the bed and closed his eyes. For a moment the rush of thoughts that came immediately upon him threatened to overwhelm him. But he stemmed and silenced them with a grim self-control. After a little while, like a soldier in the field and under arms, he slept.

Chapter 12

Daniel Wylcoxin came for him at eight-fifteen the following morning and rode along as Jim was transferred by closed car to the Committee room in one of the government buildings at Government Center. The Inquiry, Wylcoxin told him, was to start at nine.

Jim asked the other man only whether he had been able to get in touch with Ro. Wylcoxin nodded.

"They wouldn't let me out to the ship to see her," Wylcoxin said, "but I was able to talk into the ship from the guard line outside it, on a field phone they've rigged in order to keep in touch with her and that other fellow aboard. I asked her a lot of general questions, ostensibly for answers I needed in acting as your counsel, and slipped the information you wanted given her in between the lines, so to speak."

"Good," said Jim.

However, after that, and during the half-hour ride into Government Center in the closed car, Jim withdrew into himself and ignored the questions Wylcoxin put him, to the point where the other man finally got exasperated and forced himself on Jim's attention by joggling Jim's elbow.

"Look. Give me some answers, will you?" demanded Wylcoxin. "In half an hour I'm going to have to be up there, theoretically aiding and representing you as your counsel. You *owe* me some answers! Don't forget, I got through to Ro for you, and that wasn't easy. There was absolutely no line of communication open to her except that field telephone from the spaceport outside into your ship."

Jim looked at him.

"Government Center is less than ten miles from Government Center spaceport," he said; "isn't that right?"

"Why . . . yes," said Wylcoxin, wondering.

"If I'd been in a building in Government Center, I wouldn't have needed you to get in touch with Ro," said Jim. "At that distance, I could've talked directly to the ship myself."

Wylcoxin looked at him with a mixture of disbelief and puzzlement.

"I'm only pointing out," said Jim quietly, "that there's no point in my wasting valuable thinking time giving you answers you're not going to be able to understand, even if you could believe them. As far as the Committee members, Max Holland, and the other witnesses are concerned—it doesn't matter what they say, or what they ask me. All I'm

asking from you, now that you've got word
to Ro, is to sit by my side and do whatever
seems necessary as things come up."

Jim went back to his thoughts. This time
Wylcoxin left him alone with them.

They reached Government Center and the
building where the Inquiry was to take place.
Jim was kept in a small side room until just
before the Committee members were due to
appear. Then he and Wylcoxin were taken
to their seats in an already filled Committee room.

Jim and Wylcoxin were installed at one
of the several tables directly in front of the
raised platform with its long table at which
the six Committee members would sit. As
he came in, he saw, seated separately in the
crowd a few rows back from the front row
tables, Max Holland and Styrk Jacobsen—
the executive heads of the program that
had trained him to go to the Throne World—
and Ro, as well as a handful of other, minor
figures out of his past from the time when
he had been selected to be trained and sent.

Ro caught his eye, looking a little pale
and anxious, as he came in. She was dressed
in a plain white clothlike tunic and skirt,
not too remarkably different from the light-
weight, summer-colored clothes of the Earth
women seated in the same room. But some
general effect of her total appearance made
her stand out in the crowd, as if spotlighted.
Jim's eyes had adjusted to the height and
cleanliness of feature of the High-born on

the Throne World. Now, in spite of himself, the people of his own world, thronging this courtroom, seemed shrunken and small and drab by comparison. Ro, ignoring all the rest, was looking at him anxiously. Jim smiled to reassure her, as he took his seat, necessarily turning his back on her and the rest of those in seats behind him. The six Committee members came in, representatives of their various area sectors on Earth. The audience rose on order, to wait for the members to take their seats; and at the same time, a buzz of excitement ran through them, as there came in with the other members a small, reddish-brown man, who took his seat to the right of Alvin Heinman, representative from the powerful Central European sector. Jim looked at the small man and smiled faintly. But the other only looked back with extreme solemnity. The members seated themselves, and the audience was told they could regain their seats as the Committee went on to open proceedings.

". . . And let the records show," said Heinman a little nasally into the recording sensors built in the table before him, "that the Governor of Alpha Centauri III has consented to sit with this board unofficially, in order to give it the benefit of his experience and knowledge in the matter under Inquiry."

Heinman rapped on the table with the gavel and called for the government's Investigating Officer to describe the matter under Inquiry.

The Investigating Officer did so. The word "treason" was carefully avoided, but the Investigating Officer talked a clever circle around it, until there was no doubt left in the minds of those listening to him that this Inquiry had been brought to determine not whether the government should commence treason proceedings against Jim, but whether there was the slightest doubt that the government should not do so. The Investigating Officer sat down again, and Styrk Jacobsen was brought up to answer the questions of the Committee.

These questions had to do mainly with Jim's background and the procedure which had chosen him from several hundred candidates preselected on a worldwide basis to be the man trained to go to the Throne World.

". . . James Keil," Jacobsen said, "was unusually qualified in many respects. His physical condition was superb—as it needed to be, since we planned to train the man we would send to be a bullfighter. Also, at the time Jim came to our attention, he not only had degrees in history and chemistry, as well as anthropology, but he had established himself as a respectable authority in the field of social and cultural studies."

"Would you say," broke in Heinman, "in character he was markedly different from the other candidates?"

"He was a strong individualist. But then, they all were," said Jacobsen dryly. He was a spare, erect man with silver hair, in his mid-sixties, originally from Odense, Denmark. Jim remembered that Jacobsen, from the first, had taken what seemed to be an instinctive liking to him, as opposed to Max Holland's immediate, instinctive dislike.

". . . That was one of the requirements for the job," Jacobsen was saying. He went on to list, in order, those requirements as they had originally been laid out. Roughly, they covered unusual physical and mental capacity, emotional stability, and a broad educational background.

"But about this matter of emotional stability," Heinman pounced again. "Didn't you find him unusually—say—unsocial? To the point of being noncommunicative and withdrawn from the people around him? What I mean is, wasn't he from the start pretty much of a loner?"

"Yes. Again," said Jacobsen, "we wanted someone with exactly those traits. Our man would be plunged into an unfamiliar culture—much more unfamiliar than anything he could encounter here on Earth. We wanted him to be as self-sufficient as possible."

Jacobsen had not backed up a step. Though Heinman picked up the questioning for some little time, the silver-haired man refused to give ground. His testimony amounted to the fact that Jim was no more and no less than the man the Project had been set up to find, train, and send out.

With Max Holland, who followed Jacobsen before the Committee, the response was entirely different.

". . . The other members of the team engaged in the Project," Holland said, leaning forward over the table, a cigarette burning between his fingers, "weren't equipped to consider the risk involved in it—the risk to the Earth as a whole, I mean. In resources and population, our world, to the Empire, is like a baby chick to an elephant. The chick's so small that it's likely to be safe through being ignored, unless by accident or mistake it gets under one of the elephant's feet. Then there's no hope for it. It seemed to me the whole Project ran a serious danger of bringing us under one of the elephant feet of the Empire, either accidentally or by error on the part of the man we were sending in to look at their Throne World. And my uneasiness was increased by the character and attitudes of James Keil himself. . . ."

Holland, like Jacobsen, was closely questioned by Heinman and a couple of the other Committee members. Unlike Jacobsen, Holland was ready and willing to paint a dangerous picture of Jim. Jim, he testified, had struck him as being socially withdrawn to the point of near-paranoia, self-confident and arrogant to the point of near-megalomania. Then, coldly, he reported the conversation he had had with Jim underneath the stands of the arena on Alpha Centauri III, in which

Jim had told him that from then on he would have to make his own decisions.

"Then, in your opinion," said Heinman, "this man, even before he reached the Throne World, was already determined to ignore the directives given him and do whatever he chose, regardless of whatever consequences to the rest of the people of Earth that might entail?"

"I do," said Holland as fervently as any bridegroom. That ended his appearance before the Committee.

Ro was called up next. But her appearance consisted only of sitting and listening to a recording that had been made of her own account of what had happened to Jim from the time she had first met him aboard the Princess Afuan's spaceship until the time in which she had brought him back to the spaceport outside Government Center, Earth.

As the recording ended, Heinman cleared his throat and leaned forward as if to speak to her. But the Governor of Alpha Centauri III, beside him, hastily leaned over in his turn and whispered in the Committee chairman's ear. Heinman listened and then sank back in his seat. Ro was released from her interview with the Committee without any further questions.

Beside Jim, through all this, Wylcoxin had been fidgeting in his chair. Now he leaned over and spoke urgently, low-voiced to Jim.

"Look!" he said. "At least let me take

advantage of your right to cross-question her. That Alpha Centauran Governor made a mistake when he stopped Heinman from asking her questions. It may have been a kindness to her, but it wasn't any help to you. She *wants* to testify in your favor. If we get her up there, I'm sure we can make a good impression with her!"

Jim shook his head. In any case, there was no more time to argue, because now he was being called upon to answer the questions of the Committee himself. Heinman began, mildly enough, by reviewing Jim's qualifications for being sent as an observer to the Throne World. But he drifted from these almost imperceptibly into sensitive territory.

"... Did you at any time have doubts about the wisdom of this Project?" he asked Jim.

"No," said Jim.

"But at some time between your selection as the man to go and when you arrived at the Throne World, you seemed to have developed such doubts." Heinman plowed among the notes before him on the table and finally located what it was he sought. "Mr. Holland reports you as saying on Alpha Centauri III—and I quote—'... Max, it's too late for you to interfere now. I've been invited. From now on I make my own decisions.' Is that correct?"

"No," said Jim.

"No?" Heinman frowned at him over the notes he still held in his hand.

"The wording isn't correct," said Jim. "What I actually said was, 'I'm sorry, Max. But it was bound to come to this sooner or later. From here on out the Project can't guide me any longer. From now on I have to follow my own judgment.' "

Heinman's frown deepened.

"I don't see any essential difference," he said.

"Neither did Max Holland, evidently," said Jim. "But I did—or else I wouldn't have phrased it that way."

Jim felt his left sleeve below the tabletop being plucked frantically.

"Easy!" hissed the whispering voice of Wlycoxin in his ear. "For God's sake, take it easy!"

"You didn't?" said Heinman with a faint note of triumph in his voice. He sat back and looked right and left along the table at the other members of the Committee. "And do you deny taking a knife and a revolver in your luggage to the Throne World, over Mr. Holland's objections?"

"No," said Jim.

Heinman coughed dryly, took out a white handkerchief and patted his lips, then tucked the handkerchief away again and sat back in his chair.

"Well," he said. "That seems to cover that."

He reached for a fresh sheet of paper and wrote something on it in pencil.

"Now"—he began leaning forward over the table once more—"you've heard the account of your actions from the time you left Alpha Centauri III until you returned to Earth that's been given us by Miss—the High-born Ro. Have you any exception to take with that account?"

"No," said Jim.

Once more he was aware of Wylcoxin's fingers plucking at his sleeve. But he paid no attention.

"No exception," said Heinman, leaning back once more. "Then I take it you've no explanation at all for these extraordinary actions of yours, completely at odds with your original purpose in being sent to the Throne World?"

"I didn't say that," said Jim. "The account you got is correct. The interpretation of it you've made is wrong. Just as wrong as your assumption that my intentions or actions were at variance with the reason for which I was originally sent to the Throne World from Earth."

"Then you'd better explain those intentions, don't you think, Mr. Keil?" said Heinman.

"I intend to," said Jim.

The response brought a little color to Heinman's somewhat gray cheeks. But the chairman of the Committee evidently decided in favor of letting the implied challenge pass. He waved to Jim to continue.

"The explanation's simple enough," said Jim. "The High-born of the Empire's Throne World"—he glanced at the Governor—"I'm sure the Governor of Alpha Centauri III will agree with me—are quite literally superior beings, not only to what they call the lesser races on their own Colony Worlds, men like the Governor himself"—Jim glanced at the Governor, but this time the small man avoided his eye—"but to our kind of human on Earth, as well. Accordingly, any preplanning of my actions, no matter how thoroughly or capably done here on Earth, could not guide me in an unfamiliar culture of a race whose least member was more capable than our best here on Earth. So I had to face the fact early in my training that I'd have to react to situations as I found them on the Throne World, following my own best judgment and paying no attention to how I knew people back on Earth would have decided."

"You didn't tell your superiors during the training period about this decision, I take it," asked Heinman, still leaning back in his chair.

"No," answered Jim. "If I'd told them early enough in my training to be replaced, undoubtedly I'd have been replaced."

Jim heard a little explosion of breath to his left, a gusty exhalation of despair from Wylcoxin.

"Of course, of course," said Heinman pleasantly. "Go on, Mr. Keil."

"Accordingly," said Jim evenly, "when I got to the Throne World, I discovered that the best interests of Earth would be served there by involving myself in the situation about the Emperor rather than just staying an observer. The Emperor was mad, and his cousin Galyan had been conspiring for a long time to gain control over the Emperor, by eliminating the man who really ran the Empire, Vhotan—the Emperor's uncle and Galyan's also. Galyan's plan called for him to eliminate Vhotan and the Starkiens, who were unswervingly loyal to the Emperor. Then Galyan would assume Vhotan's place, take over control of the Throne World and the Empire, and develop a new corps of Starkiens, loyal not to the Emperor but to himself. The Starkiens were literally a special breed of men, created originally by gene control and controlled breeding over several generations. But Galyan knew he could produce a new breed within two or three generations, given the means and the raw material. And the raw material was to come from us—from Earth."

He stopped and looked at the Committee members behind their long table.

Chapter 13

It was a second or two after Jim had stopped talking before his last few quiet words exploded with their proper implication upon the minds of his Earth-born audience. Then the effect was, in a small way, dramatic. Heinman sat straight up. The other members of the Committee, all up and down the table, reacted with an equal and sudden alertness.

"What was that, Mr. Keil?" demanded Heinman. "You're accusing this Prince Galyan—he was one of the ones killed, wasn't he—of wanting to alter us genetically to some sort of single-minded bodyguards for his own purposes?"

"I'm not accusing him," said Jim evenly. "I'm stating a fact—the acknowledged fact of Galyan's intentions. The fact he acknowledged to me. He planned to do exactly what I say. I don't think you understand"—for the first time a little touch of irony swept into Jim's voice—"that his doing that, by itself, wouldn't have seemed so terrible to the rest of the High-born on the Throne

World. After all, the lesser breeds of humans on their Colony Worlds were available material for the High-borns' using. And we weren't even that important. We were Wolflings—wild men and women living out beyond the fringe of the civilized Empire."

Heinman leaned back and turned to whisper to the Governor of Alpha Centauri beside him. Jim sat without speaking until the whispered conversation came to an end. Heinman turned back to Jim and leaned forward. His face was slightly flushed.

"A little while earlier," Heinman said, "you told us that the High-born on the Throne World were superior beings. How can you reconcile the fact they were superior beings with such inhuman plans on the part of this Prince Galyan? Let alone the fact that, according to you, he planned to murder his uncle and dominate his Emperor? If the High-born are what you say they are—and the Governor of Alpha Centauri III, here, agrees with you, at least in that—the Prince Galyan would've been far too civilized to entertain such savage and murderous intentions."

Jim laughed.

"I still don't think you, or the other members of this Committee, understand the cultural situation between the High-born and the humans on the Colony Worlds—or us," he said. "Galyan's plan against the Emperor was an ultimate in crimes, from the viewpoint of any decent High-born, like Slothiel.

But his plans about us weren't inhuman at all, as any High-born would see it. In fact, most High-born would consider us lucky to have the benefit of Galyan's attention. In making us into Starkiens, they'd have pointed out, he'd have rid us of disease and made us a much more healthy, happy, and uniform race. Just as the Emperor's Starkiens are disease-free, happy. and uniform."

Once more Heinman held a whispered consultation with the Governor. This time when it broke off, however, both men looked annoyed and a little dissatisfied.

"Are you trying to tell us, Mr. Keil," said Heinman, and it was more of an honest, open demand for information than any of the questions the Committee chairman had asked Jim earlier, "that all the actions you took on the Throne World were justified, not merely for the good of the Emperor there, but for the good of the people of Earth back here?"

"Yes," said Jim.

"I'd like to believe you," said Heinman, and at the moment it sounded as if he actually would have liked to believe Jim. "But you're asking us to take a great deal on faith. Not the least of which is how you could come to know the plans of this Prince Galyan, when they necessarily must have been kept extremely secret."

"They were kept secret," said Jim. "Certain of the Governors and Nobles on the Colony Worlds"—his eyes lingered for a second on the Alpha Centauran Governor—"had to know about his plan to get rid of the Starkiens. The Princess Afuan and Melness, the master servant in the Throne World palace, had to know other parts. But as much as possible, Galyan told nobody but himself."

"Then how could you find out?" demanded another member of the Committee—a short-bodied, fat man in high middle age whom Jim did not recognize.

"I'm an anthropologist," said Jim dryly. "My main field of interest is human culture, in all its types and variations. And there's a certain limit to the variations that can take place in human culture, given concentrated population, no matter how advanced the culture may be. The social arrangement of the High-born on the Throne World, and the social arrangements of the Nobles on the Colony Worlds, which mirrored the Throne World arrangement, were at odds with the cultural level which the High-born themselves believed they had achieved. The High-born—and the colonial Nobles in imitation—were split into small artificial cliques or groups which operated essentially like *noyaux*."

Jim paused and waited for them to ask him what *noyaux* were. Heinman did.

"The French ethnologist Jean-Jacques Petter coined the term *noyau* as a label for a society of inward antagonism," Jim answered. "Robert Ardrey, writing some years later, identified it as a 'neighborhood of territorial proprietors bound together by a dear-enemy relationship.' The Callicebus monkey is an example of the *noyau* in nature. Each Callicebus family spends its time, apart from eating and sleeping, in going to the borders of that territory which they had marked out for their own among the general treetops and engaging in screaming and threatening with the adjoining family of Callicebus, who have also come to their boundary so that the display of antagonism can take place. This, except for the fact that physical territory was replaced by 'position' and screaming and threats were replaced by intrigue to make the next person or group lose status among his fellows, exemplifies the *noyau*-like situation existing among the High-born on the Throne World. The only ones exempt from it were those like the High-born Ro, because she was an atavism—a throwback at a time when the High-born specialized physical and mental type was not yet fully developed—and therefore the others considered her not able to compete. . . . Although, she was."

Jim paused again. For a moment no one on the Committee said anything. Then Heinman spoke again.

"A little earlier," he said, "you were likening these High-born to superior beings, compared to us here on Earth. Now you're comparing them to a society of monkeys. They can't be both."

"Oh, yes, they can," said Jim. "Ardrey

also made the statement that 'nations produce heroes, *noyaux* geniuses.' In the case
of the Throne World, which set the pattern
for the colonial Governors and Nobles, the
process was reversed. Geniuses made *noyaux*.
The Callicebus monkey lives in what is essentially a utopia. Food and drink are right
at hand for him on the trees. Just so, the
High-born on the Throne World also lived
in a utopia where their technology took care
of every possible physical need or want they
could have. Normally, under utopian conditions, they should have grown soft and become easy prey to the members of the human race on the Colony Worlds who did
not have it quite so soft. That's the histori-
cal turnover of society, in which an aristocracy weakens and becomes supplanted by
those from below."

"Why didn't it happen with the High-
born?" asked Heinman.

"Because they succeeded in achieving
something unique—a practical, self-perpetuating aristocracy," said Jim. "The Empire
began by pooling all its best minds on the
planet that was later to become the Throne
World. When it became the Throne World,
it still drew to it anyone of unusual talent
who appeared on any of the other worlds.
This gave it a small trickle, a small but
continuous supply, of new blood. In addi-
tion to this, the aristocracy that developed
on the Throne World and became the High-
born did something earlier aristocracies

never were able to do. It required each member of the aristocracy to know everything there was to know about the technology that made the Empire work. In other words, the High-born were not merely pan-geniuses, they were pan-authorities. The High-born Ro, behind me now, given time, materials, and labor, could turn the Earth into a complete small duplicate of the Empire in every technological respect."

Heinman frowned.

"I don't see the connection between this, and they're being *noyaux*," the chairman said.

"An indefinitely self-perpetuating aristocracy," said Jim, "runs counter to the instinctive process of human evolution. In effect, it creates an artificial situation in which social, and therefore individual, evolution can't take place. Such an aristocracy, while it can't be destroyed from the outside, therefore has to end up destroying itself. In short—the High-born after certain lengths of time had no alternative than to begin to become decadent. And they are decadent."

The Governor leaned over urgently to whisper in Heinman's ear. But Heinman shrugged him off almost angrily.

". . . As soon as I realized they were decadent," said Jim, keeping his eye not only on Heinman, but on the Governor, "I realized that the seeds of the destruction of their Empire were already sown. The *noyaux* into which their social patterns had degen-

erated were evidence of that decadence. In
other words, within a few centuries at most,
the Empire would start to break up, and no
one there would have any time to bother
with us back here on Earth. Unfortunately,
at the same time, I discovered Galyan's plan
to seize power for himself. Not all the High-
born were ideally satisfied by the outlet the
noyaux gave their emotions and hungers. A
few individuals—like Galyan, and Slothiel,
and Vhotan—wanted and needed the real
thing in the matter of conflict and victory,
rather than the shadow of its substance,
which the bickering between the *noyaux* and
the Game of Points offered them. Also,
Galyan was dangerous. Like the Emperor,
he was mad—but he was *effectively* mad,
the kind of man who could put his madness
to practical use, in contrast to his cousin.
And Galyan had plans for Earth. He would
have sucked us into the decadence of the
Empire, before the Empire had time to col-
lapse of its own weight."

Jim paused. He felt a sudden longing to
look around at Ro, to see how she was taking this revelation. But he dared not turn.

"So," he said, "I set out to stop and destroy Galyan—and I did."

He stopped speaking. The Committee
members at the table, the Governor, even
the people sitting silent in the room behind
him, continued to stay noiseless and unmoving for several seconds, as if they expected
him to continue talking. Finally a slow stir

along the line of the Committee members signaled their recognition of the fact that he was through.

"And so that's your explanation," said Heinman, slowly leaning forward and peering directly at Jim. "You did what you did to save Earth from a decadent madman. But, how do you know you were right?"

"I'll tell you," said Jim. He smiled a little grimly. "Because I found enough evidence in the records on the Throne World to satisfy me that Earth was, in fact, originally colonized by the Empire—by a party including several High-born, as they were just beginning to be called. And"—he hesitated, then said the words very slowly but clearly— *"I myself am a throwback to those High-born colonists, just as Ro is a throwback. I am a High-born. Otherwise I couldn't have done what I did, in competition with Galyan and the other High-born. I was a throwback to an earlier, healthier version of their aristocracy, and I'd look it even more than I do now if it hadn't been for the treatments that were given me here on Earth to stop my growth when I was ten years old!"*

In the silence following this remark, Jim turned and looked squarely at the Governor. The Governor sat as if frozen, his mouth a little open, his brown eyes staring fixedly at Jim. In one sweep, Jim felt the audience's sympathy and belief in himself, that had been building all during his explanation— even among the Committee members, even in Heinman himself—swept away by a cooling reaction of incredulity and distrust.

"High-born? You?" said Heinman in a low voice, staring at him.

It was almost as if the chairman questioned himself. For a long moment he continued to stare at Jim; then he shook himself back into self-control. Clearly he remembered who he was and where he was.

"That's hard to believe," he said, and his voice had the same note of faint underlying sarcasm that had been in it at the beginning of his questioning of Jim. "What kind of proof have you got to back up such a claim?"

Jim nodded quietly at the Governor of Alpha Centauri III.

"The Governor knows the High-born," said Jim, his eyes fixed on the small man. "Not only that, but he saw me on the Throne World in the midst of the native High-born there. He should be able to tell you whether I am one or not. . . . That is, provided you'll accept his evidence?"

"Oh," said Heinman, not only leaning back, but tilting back a little in his chair. "I think we can accept the Governor's opinion." He turned to the small figure beside him and asked, loudly enough for the room to hear, "Mr. Keil claims to be one of the High-born. What do you think, Governor?"

The Governor's eyes stared fixedly at Jim. He opened his mouth, hesitated, and spoke, thickly accenting the Earth-born words.

"No, no," he said. "He is not a High-born. He could never be a High-born. No . . . *No!*"

A sort of low gasp, a groan of reaction, trembled through the audience behind Jim. Jim rose slowly to his feet and folded his arms.

"Sit down, Mr. Keil!" snapped Heinman. But Jim ignored him.

"Adok!" he said, addressing the empty air.

Suddenly Adok was with them, standing in front of Jim's table, in the little clear space between it and the raised platform on which stood the table of the Committee members. He stood silent, his powerful body darkly gleaming a little under the lights, white power bands stark on his arms, body, and legs.

There was a new, shuddering gasp from the rest of the room. Then silence.

Jim turned and pointed at one long wall of the room.

"Adok," he said. "That's an outside wall. I want you to open it up. I don't want any falling debris or undue heat. I just want it opened."

Adok turned a little toward the wall Jim indicated. The Starkien did not seem to move, otherwise, but there was a wink of light that seemed brilliant enough to blind them all, if it had not been for the extremely short duration of its existence; and something like an unbearable sound, equally cut short.

Where the wall had been there was an irregular opening ten feet in height, fifty feet in length, and with edges smoothly rounded, as if the stone of the wall had been melted.

Through the opening they could see, over the rooftops of a few adjoining buildings, blue sky in which half a dozen cloud masses floated. Jim pointed at the sky.

"Those clouds, Adok," he said, softly. "Take them away."

There were five or six short, whistling noises—again like mighty sounds cut so short that the human ear did not suffer from hearing them.

The sky was clear.

Jim turned back to face the table on the raised platform. Slowly he raised his arm and pointed at the Governor of Alpha Centauri III.

"Adok—" he began. The squat brown figure came hurdling over the table before him, down off the platform, and across the table to Jim himself, reaching out his hands supplicatingly.

"*No, no, High-born!*" cried the Governor in the language of the Empire. Then, desperately, he switched to English.

"No!" he shouted, twisting his head sideways to look back over his shoulder at the members of the Committee. His voice in its thickly accented speech rang wildly against the silence of the room. "I was wrong! Wrong! He *is* High-born. I tell you, he is!"

The Governor's voice rose frantically, for Heinman and the other Committee members were staring at him with expressions of mixed horror and disbelief. He twisted around on the tabletop to confront them.

"No, no!" he cried thickly. "I don't say that because he pointed at me. No! It's because of the Starkien! You don't understand! The Starkiens obey nobody but the Emperor and those other High-born the Emperor tells the Starkiens to obey. The Starkien couldn't obey like that for anybody but a High-born! It's true! He *is* High-born, and I was wrong! I was wrong! You have to treat him like a High-born! Because he *is!*"

The Governor collapsed into a fit of hysterical weeping, huddled up on the tabletop. Jim felt a hand slide into his own, and looking down, saw that Ro had come from her seat to stand at his side.

"Yes, indeed," Ro said slowly in careful but unpracticed English, to Heinman. "I am a High-born, and I tell you that Jim is one too. The Emperor adopted him as one, but even the Emperor said that he was giving Jim nothing Jim did not already have. Jim risked his life for all of you, and he brought me and Adok back to make you a people who will someday inherit the Empire."

She stopped and turned to point to the sobbing Governor.

"This man," she said, "must have been one of the colonials in Galyan's plot. He sent a stone from Earth in Jim's name. Only it was not a stone, but a device to project a blue, distorting light over Vhotan; and when it did this, the poor Emperor thought he saw the Blue Beast of his nightmares, and was so afraid that he ordered Vhotan killed, just as Galyan had planned. Wasn't it this man who suggested you should try Jim for treason?"

"I lied. I told them the Princess Afuan would shortly remove the High-born Slothiel, and then she would seek payment from Earth for what Jim had done," moaned the Governor, swaying on the table with his face hid in his hands. "But I was wrong—*wrong!* He *is* High-born. Not just by adoption, but by birth. I was wrong, wrong. . . ."

On Heinman's face there was a war of expressions, but gradually dominating them all came the look of a man who had just emerged from many miles of dark tunnels to find a daylight so much brighter than he had expected that it was almost too painful to bear.

Jim looked at him, then nodded down at the weeping Governor before returning his eyes grimly to Heinman once more.

"Yes," Jim said. "So now you understand. . . . And you can also understand why the Empire was something to be kept from Earth, at any cost."

YOU

CAN WIN

$10,000

BUT ONLY IF YOU TAKE . . .

What would you do if you discovered that the President of the United States was a Soviet spy? That's the incredible situation faced by Larry Fox, lower-echelon CIA agent in Istanbul, in *Active Measures*, the first science fiction/espionage novel to offer a $10,000 prize! Complete details appear in every copy of *Active Measures*, a Baen Book by Janet Morris and David Drake. But *Active Measures* isn't just a chance to win a large cash prize—it's also a gripping, action-filled story.

Here's just a taste to get you started:

"You wanted an hour," Gallen reminded him. "You've got fifty-three minutes left." She reached up and fitted the tab of the door's chain bolt into its slot. The snick of metal on metal was no harder than her blue eyes.

"Check. I interviewed a Soviet defector who appeared to be . . . *could be*—" Fox said bluntly as he eased to the foot of the bed and sat facing the side wall rather than the woman by the door—"Abdulhamid Kunayev." The bolt above her head wouldn't hold a solid kick: it provided a symbol of the bargain Gallen had accepted; lighting a long fuze would have done the same. "In the course of the interview, the defector stated that President Crossfield is a Soviet penetration." Listening to himself, Fox realized how crazy he sounded and began quickly to explain: "He—"

She cut him off: "What evidence did this . . . defector . . . cite to support those statements?" Her voice was emotionless but it seemed to have risen an octave.

"Captain, I didn't *believe* them," Fox said despairingly in a low voice that trembled. There was a mirror over the long desk built into the wall opposite the bed; he closed his eyes rather than stare at his own face, battered by weakness and failure. The implications of the Kunayev contact were too important for validation to depend solely on him; but nobody was going to make decisions based on the information he'd collected until and unless he could convince Shai Gallen that there was some decision to make concerning Larry Fox, GS-11, Field Collector of moderate experience, beyond how deep under Langley to bury him.

He didn't know how in hell to begin doing that, but he realized as he monitored his thoughts that at least he was worried about it—human again, with human feelings, not just a computing gunsight—though somewhere in him that gunsight was locked onto his memories like a targeting array, waiting for someone to squeeze the red switch.

"Sir," Fox said a little too loudly as he attempted to override the quaver in his voice, "the defector broke contact almost at once." Gallen wasn't a girl he'd known in the Lebanon; she was his DDO—operations director for CIA; he *had* to handle this like the professional he ought to be. "He said he was afraid of the U.S. because the President was a mole, then he took off as if he saw something in the street below. I was prevented from following him by my Turkish contact. So I didn't see what happened—I lost contact with the defector."

Gallen got up from the armchair with a look of cold fury on her face. Her glasses didn't distort the glaring eyes behind them: the lenses were clear, an excuse for the heavy frames. Fox was willing to bet that the attache case beside the DDO held at least a recorder and a voice-stress analyzer. Gallen's glasses would house either an actual intercom connecting her to a crew outside the room, or an audio monitor giving her a readout from the stress analyzer. The tone in Gallen's ear would change as the level of stress in Fox's voice went up and down. There were more reasons for stress than the subject choosing to lie, however; he hoped she'd remember that.

Abruptly Gallen slammed the wall behind her with the side of her fist: "Give me some *reason* that a man with Kunayev's resources would pick a low-level line operative to tell his story to ... some reason not to think you're feeding me crap which, based on the increased message traffic and troop movements on the Sino-Soviet and NATO borders, the Soviets know damn well that Blaustein's Assessment boys would love to believe. Come *on*, Larry—*find* something. Even you've got to realize that you're dead in the water if I can't help you and that I *won't* help you if it puts my credibility, and therefore hundreds of my field operators, in jeopardy. If anybody's going to get fucked here tonight, it's you, not me. We're not talking about flow-charts now, we're talking about extended chemical debriefing." Her fist uncurled and her hand cut a tight, angry circle in the air.

Fox looked at her and took a deep breath. . . .